D0467138

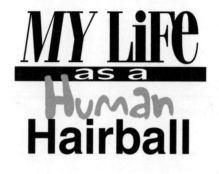

MY LiFe
as a
Human
Hairball

Tommy Nelson® Books by Bill Myers

Series

SECRET AGENT DINGLEDORF
. . . and his trusty dog, SPLAT

The Case of the . . .

Giggling Geeks • Chewable Worms
• Flying Toenails • Drooling Dinosaurs •
Hiccupping Ears • Yodeling Turtles

The Incredible Worlds of Wally McDoogle

My Life As . . .

a Smashed Burrito with Extra Hot Sauce • Alien Monster Bait
• a Broken Bungee Cord • Crocodile Junk Food •
Dinosaur Dental Floss • a Torpedo Test Target
• a Human Hockey Puck • an Afterthought Astronaut •
Reindeer Road Kill • a Toasted Time Traveler
• Polluted Pond Scum • a Bigfoot Breath Mint •
a Blundering Ballerina • a Screaming Skydiver
• a Human Hairball • a Walrus Whoopee Cushion •
a Computer Cockroach (Mixed-Up Millennium Bug)
• a Beat-Up Basketball Backboard • a Cowboy Cowpie •
Invisible Intestines with Intense Indigestion
• a Skysurfing Skateboarder • a Tarantula Toe Tickler •
a Prickly Porcupine from Pluto • a Splatted-Flat Quarterback
• a Belching Baboon • a Stupendously Stomped Soccer Star •

IMAGER CHRONICLES

The Portal • *The Experiment* • *The Whirlwind* • *The Tablet*

Picture Book

Baseball for Breakfast

www.Billmyers.com

the incredible worlds of **Wally McDoogle**

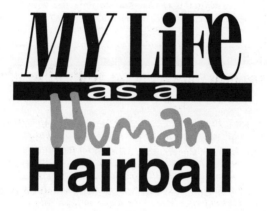

MY LiFe
as a
Human
Hairball

B I L L   M Y E R S

Tommy
NELSON

A Division of Thomas Nelson Publishers
Since 1798

www.thomasnelson.com

MY LIFE AS A HUMAN HAIRBALL
Copyright © 1998 by Bill Myers

Published in Nashville, Tennessee, by Tommy Nelson®, a Division of Thomas Nelson, Inc. Visit us on the Web at www.tommynelson.com

Library of Congress Cataloging-in-Publication Data

Myers, Bill, 1953–
    My life as a human hairball / Bill Myers.
       p. cm. — (The incredible worlds of Wally McDoogle ; 15)
    Summary: Accidentally miniaturized in a lab, thirteen-year-old Wally and his friend Wall Street travel through the inside of a person's body, viewing his anatomy and marveling at the wonders of God's creation.
    ISBN-10: 0-8499-4024-9
    ISBN-13: 978-0-8499-4024-8
    [1. Body, Human—Fiction. 2. Science—Experiments—Fiction. 3. Christian life—Fiction. 4. Humorous stories.]
I. Title. II. Series: Myers, Bill, 1953- . Incredible worlds of Wally McDoogle ; #15.
PZ7.M98234M1 1998
[Fic]—dc21
                                        98-7219
                                         CIP
                                         AC

Printed in the United States of America

07 08 09 10 RRD 18 17 16 15 14 13 12

To Tina Shuman—
for her resourcefulness and commitment.

"I praise you because I am wonderfully and fearfully made . . ."

Psalm 139:14 (NIV)

Contents

Chapter 1

Just for Starters . . .

The next time I say God is boring, just tape my mouth shut, throw me off the World Trade Center, or get me a brain transplant (because it's obvious I've lost my mind). What I learned just about His creativity and how He puts the human body together is enough to write an entire book, which— come to think about it—I'm doing.

It all started with another boring field trip, to another boring science place, courtesy of our boring science teacher, Mr. Reptenson. I don't want to be too hard on the guy, but if you ever have trouble going to sleep, just swing by one of his lectures and you'll be snoozing away in seconds.

Only instead of listening to Mr. Reptenson, we were listening to some research guy who wore more pocket protectors than our entire chess club put together. At the moment he was droning on about the laboratory we were visiting—how they make those little video cameras that go into the human body to see what's happening inside. Talk about interesting. It was so exciting that the entire class had broken out into a bad case of the yawns.

But then, just as I was mastering the fine art of sleepwalking, we headed into this giant room with a huge machine that stretched all the way to the ceiling. Directly below it was some sort of minisubmarine mounted on a platform.

"What's that?" Opera, my best friend, shouted over his Walkman. Opera is always shouting something over his Walkman—usually it's "Where's the dip?" (The only thing he likes better than listening to Mozart is scarfing down multiple bags of potato chips.)

"This is our latest experiment," Mr. Pocket Protector beamed.

I took another swig from my can of soda and actually found myself starting to listen.

"We're just in the beginning stages," he explained, "but someday we hope to miniaturize that submarine with the help of this Molecular Compressor Miniaturizer." He slapped his hand against the giant machine that towered above us. "When that happens, we'll be able to make the submarine small enough to actually enter the human body. Then we'll be able to rove about making repairs from the inside."

"Hold the phone," Wall Street interrupted (she's my other best friend—even if she is a girl). "You mean this giant machine, this Molecular Whatchamacallit, can actually make things smaller?"

"That's right."

"Wow," Opera exclaimed. "Just like that movie, *Honey, I Shrunk My Underwear?*" (Opera doesn't get out all that often.)

"Well, sort of," the man said. "It's still very much in the experimental stage, but someday we hope to put it to work. Now, if you'll step with me into this next room, I'll show you a fantastic video clip on the latest advances in optical enhancement."

Everyone groaned as we started forward. Well, everyone but Wall Street.

"Pssst," she whispered. "Hey, Wally?"

I threw a look over my shoulder. She was hanging toward the back of the group motioning for me to join her.

I slowed down. "What's up?" I asked.

She glanced around and lowered her voice even more. "I don't know about you, but the last thing in the world I want to do is watch another boring video."

I nodded. "Tell me about it."

She continued to slow our walk until we were at the very back of the group.

"What are you doing?" I asked.

She motioned for me to keep my voice down. "Let's stay in here and check out this cool stuff."

"We can't do that!"

"Says who?" By now most of the class had entered the other room. "It'll only be for a couple of minutes," she insisted. "We'll catch up to them before they're done. They'll never miss us."

I knew we should stay with the group, but when it comes to watching boring videos or checking out fancy minisubmarines with even fancier sci-fi Miniaturizing Machines . . . well, you can see my problem. Besides, it's not like we were doing anything wrong. I mean it's not my fault we just happen to be extra slow walkers—or that we just happened to duck out of sight when Mr. Pocket Protector poked his head in and checked for stragglers. And it's not my fault that he shut the door behind him with a loud

K-THUD.

But there we were, all alone . . . just the minisubmarine, the machine, and my guilty conscience.

"Come on." Wall Street motioned for me to hop over the railing and head on down to the submarine. I hesitated, then reluctantly followed. That was my second mistake. Unfortunately, there would be plenty more to come.

The submarine was pretty small, about ten feet long. It was mounted on a wooden cradle that held it a couple of feet off the floor. Wall Street was the first to arrive. She pressed her face against one of the windows and took a look. A moment later I had joined her. Inside, we could see two seats, a whole bunch of video screens, and more wires than the back of our VCR after Dad is done trying to hook it up.

"Cool," Wall Street half whispered.

I nodded. When she was right, she was right. Unfortunately, she could also be wrong. Before I knew it, she had found the ladder leading up to the open hatch and started climbing it.

"Wall Street," I said, "what are you doing? Get down!"

"Why? What's the big deal?"

"The big deal is, we shouldn't even be here."

"I'm just going to take a peek inside."

"Wall Street, don't . . ."

But she had already reached the top and was poking her head down into it. "Wow! You gotta check this out."

"I'm not checking anything out." I folded my arms across my chest to prove I meant business. Now, she knew I was mad. Now, she knew I was serious. Now, she turned around and climbed down inside.

"WALL STREET!" I yelled.

She appeared at the inside window and waved to me.

"Get out of there!" I cried. "Wall Street!"

But she refused to take me seriously. (Why should she start now?) Instead, she turned around and began checking out all the cool instruments.

"Wall Street!"

Ditto in the no respect department.

I had to do something, I had to get her out of there before we were caught. With the world's second biggest sigh (the biggest will come up on page 9), I carefully scooted my pop can under the submarine so it wouldn't get kicked over, and I started up the ladder after her.

The good news was I only slipped and fell a half-dozen times (climbing ladders can be risky to the coordinationally challenged). When I finally got to the top, I stuck my head inside and called, "Let's go. Come on. Wall Street, don't make me come down there after you."

She looked up from a bunch of video screens and grinned. "You've got to see this."

"See what?"

"There's this cool panel here. Looks like a remote control to that Miniaturizing Machine above us."

I didn't feel like climbing down to see it, but I didn't exactly feel like missing out either. So I did the next best thing. I stuck my head down a little farther into the hatch. Unfortunately, a video monitor blocked my view so I stuck it down a little farther. And then a little farther. And then—

Suddenly I'd run out of little farthers. Come to think of it, I'd also run out of open hatches.

"AUGH!"
K-Thunk . . . K-Thunk . . . K-Thunk . . .

The "AUGH!" was me falling head first through the hatch. (And you thought I was kidding about being coordinationally challenged.) The *K-Thunk . . . K-Thunk . . . K-Thunk* was the sound of my head catching every rung of the ladder as I fell.

Unfortunately, those were the good sounds. There were also a few bad ones—like me crashing into Wall Street:

"OAFF!"

"Sorry . . ."
And her screaming as she lost her balance:

"WALLY!"
Stagger . . . stagger . . . stagger. . .
"LET GO OF . . ."
Stumble . . . stumble . . . stumble . . .
". . . ME!!"

Next up was the ever popular:

K-SLAM!

as we smashed into the fancy control panel. This was immediately followed by the

K-RACKLE K-RACKLE K-RACKLE
SIZZLE SIZZLE SIZZLE
POP POP POP

of the control panel shorting out.

There were more sparks than when our cat Collision gnaws on the light cord. More smoke than when it's my little sister's night to cook.

But we still weren't done. That would be too easy. There was still one last little sound.

WOZZA-WOZZA-WOZZA-WOZZA-WOZZA

"What's that?" Wall Street cried.

"I don't know!" I said, coughing and waving the smoke out of my face. I staggered to the window to take a look.

"What do you see?" she yelled over the noise.

"Nothing. Just some red beam shooting out of that giant machine above us."

"What red beam?" She quickly joined me.

"The one coming out of that Miniaturizer Machine and hitting our submarine."

She let out the world's loudest sigh (see I told you there was one louder than page 6). I looked at Wall Street and Wall Street looked at me. Then we both said what the other was thinking:

"Uh-oh."

We glanced back outside.

"Say, Wally? Why is everything around the submarine getting bigger?"

It was true—the walls, the machine, the whole room seemed to be growing bigger. Unfortunately, you didn't have to be a rocket scientist to figure out what was really going on. It wasn't that everything was getting bigger . . .

It was that we were getting smaller!

Once again we looked at each other and once again we said what the other was thinking. Only this time, it was just a little different and just a little louder:

"AUGHHHHHHHH!"

Chapter 2

A New Weight-Loss Program

But the fun and games weren't exactly over. As we continued to shrink, the wooden cradle holding the submarine seemed to grow bigger and bigger . . . until we were so small (or it was so big) that we finally slipped through one of the cracks and fell. The good news was we got to do what we did best:

"AUGH!"

The bad news was that by our new standard of smallness the ground was at least a hundred feet below. No problem except for the part of being smashed to smithereens on the lab floor. We braced ourselves, preparing for the worst. But the worst never happened. (That comes a little later.)

Instead of slamming onto the floor, instead of the deafening crash of broken minisubmarines (and broken kids) . . . we were only jarred slightly as we heard a very odd

K-PLOP!

Wall Street looked at me and blinked. "What was that?"

I looked at her and blinked. "Got me."

We headed over to the window and looked out. To my surprise, the lab was nowhere to be seen. Instead, we were surrounded by some sort of brown, bubbling liquid. And off in the distance was what looked like a wall. But not the lab wall. This one formed a circle around us and was smooth and shiny, almost like it was metal or something.

"Where are we?" I whispered.

Wall Street shook her head. "It's definitely not Kansas, Toto."

I'll spare you the details on how heroically we behaved. Let's just say that after all the screaming, shouting, and banging on the side of the submarine for help, we finally got a grip and started to check out the place.

Actually, it was pretty cool. I mean, everywhere you looked there was your basic, state-of-the-art, sci-fi stuff—everything from navigation computers with 3-D holographic readouts to diving suits with built-in intercoms to—well, let's just say that the place was definitely high-tech in a *Star Trek* sort of way.

It didn't take long for us to get back to the source of our problem: the miniaturizer machine's remote control panel. (Actually, the source of our problem was me! Of course, we haven't been able to fix that for thirteen years, so why try now?) The point is, there had to be some way to reverse the effects of the machine so we could get back to our normal size (or even a few inches taller so I could finally stop being the school punching bag). Unfortunately, my little crash and burn routine had managed to break all the important switches and dials. (Hey, if a disaster is worth doing, it's worth doing well.) The only thing that seemed to be working was a digital clock above the control panel. But even that was running backward. At the moment it read:

22 MINUTES : 33 SECONDS

"What do you suppose that is?" I asked.

Wall Street squinted at the label underneath the time display and read it: *"Total Miniaturization Time ."*

With genius-like thinking, I opened my mouth and shared the deep thoughts running through my mind. "Huh?"

"I think that clock tells us how much time we've got left being small," she said. "You know, how much time we've got before we grow back to our normal size."

I glanced at the readout. It now said:

22 MINUTES : 25 SECONDS

I felt a wave of relief wash over me. "If that's true, then we don't have anything to worry about. All we have to do is wait around for twenty-two minutes, and we'll be back to normal."

Wall Street began to nod. "I don't want this to be a shock, but you just might be right." (There's a first time for everything.)

With nothing else to do but wait, I started poking around the submarine again. Pretty soon, I stumbled upon the keyboard to the onboard computer. Normally, to kill time and help me relax, I write stories on my laptop, Ol' Betsy. But since I didn't have her with me, and since there was nothing else happening, I plopped down in front of the computer and snapped it on. After finding the word processing program, I began to type. I was in a pretty weird place and could stand a little relaxation. Unfortunately, sometimes the weirder the place is, the weirder my story becomes . . .

It's been another sensationally super day of superherohood for the gorgeously good-looking and humongously handsome Mirror Man. Already he has straightened one of his hairs that the wind has nearly mussed, polished his teeth a half-dozen times to keep them at their sparkly best, and discovered a zit that was (gasp of gasps) just about to appear on the side of his nose. If it wasn't for his stage makeup, things might have gotten ugly. (Just don't let his superhero buddies know he uses the stuff. Okay?)

No one is certain how Mirror Man became so concerned about his reflection. Some say it was because he had grown up with too many sisters always hogging the bathroom mirror. Others insist it came from brain damage when he tried imitating Alice in Wonderland (walking through real mirrors can be a lot more painful than the storybook ones). Then there's the ever-popular theory that as a perfectionist the only image he could possibly fall in love with was his own.

Whatever the reason, our hero is never able to pass a mirror without checking himself out—for four or five hours at a time. The good news is he always looks great in case he's photographed for the cover of any famous superhero magazines. The bad news is he's so busy looking great that he never has time to do anything great to get into those magazines.

Fortunately that's all about to change. As he stands at one of his hundreds of mirrors, emptying another one of his hundreds of cans of hairspray, suddenly, the earth stops rotating! (Don't you just hate it when that happens?) In fact, it stops so abruptly that our varnish-haired hero is thrown against the wall in a major, crash-dummy-through-the-windshield kind of way:

K-SMASH!

Filled with alarm, he staggers to his feet and desperately races back to the mirror. The good news is that not a single one of his hairs is out of place. The bad news is the earth starts up again, only this time in reverse. Suddenly Mirror Man is thrown into the opposite wall.

K-SMASH!

Now our hero is really upset. Don't get me wrong, he likes playing Ping-Pong as much as the next guy—he's just not crazy about being the ball. But there's another little problem. In all of his superhero days he has never heard the sound: K-SMASH! Sure, there have been plenty of *K-RASHES!, K-BANGS!,* and even the ever-popular *K-POW!*—but never a K-SMASH!

What on earth is going on?

Suddenly our incredibly intellectual hero suspects an inconsistency. (Looks like it's time to crack open the ol' dictionary again.) Anxious to find out what happened, he races to the TV and turns on a late-breaking news bulletin.

ABZ's anchorman, Peter Jerkings is already on the air, giving a report. But for some reason, he is impossible to understand. Our hero leans forward to hear better:

"To recap our story, apparently the earth has reversed its rotation and is now spinning backward."

Suddenly they cut to a commercial break with some guy in a suit and briefcase running backward to catch a bus...that is also running backward...along with the rest of the traffic. Come to think of it, the music is playing backward, too.

But before our heartbreakingly handsome hero has any hint of what's happening (say that seven times fast), the TV picture breaks up and the remarkably revolting and repugnantly repulsive (Translation: "Majorly Ugly") RetroRunt appears on the screen.

"Greetings, Mirror Man. Or should I say, 'Greetings, Mirror Man,'?"

Our hero gasps a manly gasp. "RetroRunt?" he shouts. "What's going on? Are you the cause of all this chaos?"

"Of course," the little guy squeaks. "I've tied retrorockets all around the earth and fired them to reverse the earth's rotation."

"Is that why everything's running backward?" Mirror Man cries.

"You guessed it."

"But you can't do that!" our hero shouts.

"And why not?"

"Manipulating time was Time Trickster's plan back in book number seven. You can't ripoff another villain's gimmick."

"I'm not ripping off anything. I have no desire to twist time. Once we return to this morning, I'll release the earth and let it continue its normal spin—until tonight, when I'll reverse it again. Until it's this morning, and then again, and again some more."

"But why?"

"To keep living this day forever!"

"But you can't do that!" our hero shouts.

"You've already said that."

"But why?"

"You've already said that, too."

Even though quoting himself is almost as much fun as looking at himself, Mirror Man tries a new tact. "How come I'm not affected?" he demands. "How come I'm not living backward?"

"Because you—my grotesquely gorgeous geek—have spent your entire life looking into mirrors. You are used to seeing things in reverse. In fact, you are the only one on the planet who can stop me."

"You don't mean..." (Ta-ta-daaa!—
That's supposed to be dramatic music.)

"That's right," RetroRunt replies.
"Everyone is doomed to live this day
over and over again...unless you decide
to help them by saving the day!"

"Great Scott, you don't mean..." (TA-TA-
DAAAA—that's even more dramatic music.)

"That's right. You'll actually have to
leave your mirror and try to stop me."

"And if I don't?"

"Then the entire planet will be forced
to relive this day forever!"

Our hero gasps a gorgeously good-looking
gasp. Holy Handsomeness, what will he do?
How will he save the world from reliving
the same day over and over? More importantly, where can he find a full-length
mirror easy enough to carry with him?

These and other mildly moronic questions race through his head, when—

"Wally . . . are you guys there!? Wall Street!?
Can anybody hear me!?"

I looked up from the computer to the main video
display at the front of the submarine. There was
Opera's face filling the screen.

"Can anybody hear me?" he shouted.

I turned to Wall Street with relief. "We're found!" I shouted. "We're saved."

But before she could answer, the entire submarine lurched forward. We began pitching back and forth. Wall Street started screaming. (I would have joined her, but it's hard screaming when you're busy reminding God of all the good things you've done just in case you're about to meet Him.)

Everything was topsy-turvy in an electric blender kind of way. One minute we were on the ceiling of the submarine, the next on the floor.

I wasn't sure what was happening, but when I caught a glimpse through the window, it looked just as turbulent outside as it felt inside. It was impossible to tell what was going on or where we were going . . . but we were definitely going there way too fast!

Chapter 3

Digesting the Facts

After several more seconds, our private little wash-and-tumble cycle finally came to an end. It looked like things were finally getting back to normal. Well, normal except for the fact that we were still miniaturized people in a miniaturized submarine floating in . . . I looked out the window to check. We were no longer floating in brown bubbles. Instead it was some sort of clear, pinkish liquid.

But that wasn't the only difference.

Wall Street gave me a nudge. "Check it out."

I turned to the opposite window and saw what looked like the world's biggest potato chip. It floated outside the submarine and stretched on for dozens of yards. Not only that, but the clear liquid we were floating in seemed to be slowly eating away at the chip and turning it into liquid.

"Pretty gross, huh?"

I nodded, but before I could say anything we heard:

"Wally! Wall Street? Can you guys hear me!?"

We spun back to the front video screen. Opera was still on it, and he was still trying to get our attention. "Guys? Are you there!?"

"Opera!" I shouted. "Where are you? Opera!"

"Wally?"

"Opera?"

"Wally?"

We would have gone on like that a few more hours, but Wall Street figured it wouldn't hurt to start a real conversation. "Opera," she cried, "just tell us where you are!"

"I'm back here in the lab. At some sort of communications desk. I came back in to find you guys, but no one was here. Where are you?"

"We're in the submarine," I shouted.

He looked around. "It's not here," he yelled. "Where did you take it?"

"We didn't take it anywhere," I shouted. "It took us!"

"*What??*"

Wall Street tried to explain. "You know that big Miniaturization Machine there in the room?"

"Yeah."

"Well, I think we sorta accidentally turned it on and got ourselves accidentally miniaturized."

"You what!?! That's impossible. No one could be that klutzy!"

"But Wally is with me."

"Oh, yeah. I see your point."

She continued. "Listen, you said you're at a communications desk?"

"Yup, there's all sorts of cool video screens and stuff here."

"I'm wondering, is there any type of like . . . tracking device? You know, something that might show where the submarine is."

"Hard to say, there's so many displays . . ."

Wall Street nodded. "But if they plan to send this into human bodies some day, there's gotta be a way to keep track of it."

Opera shook his head. "I don't see anything. There's nothing but . . . oh, wait a minute."

Wall Street and I exchanged glances.

"That's weird."

"What's weird?" I asked.

"There's this giant outline of the human body. You know with the digestive system and blood vessels and everything, and . . ."

"And?" Wall Street asked.

"Well, there's a green flashing light that kinda looks like a submarine, and . . ."

"And?" I asked.

"Well, it's flashing and . . ."

"*And!?*" we both shouted.

"And it looks like it's inside the body's stomach."

"Inside the body's stomach!" I spun back to the window. Could that be where we were? Could all this liquid be inside somebody's stomach? I looked over to the giant potato chip. To my amazement it was nearly completely dissolved.

Unfortunately, that wasn't the only thing dissolving.

I tried to shout. I tried to warn Wall Street, but my heart was too busy leaping into my throat to get out any words.

"How could that happen?" Wall Street continued talking with Opera. "How could we have gotten inside somebody's stomach?"

I cleared my throat trying to get her attention. Still no luck.

"I dunno," Opera answered, "but that's what this diagram shows. It shows that you're right in the middle of—wait a minute, there's another light that just came on."

"Uh, excuse me . . . ," I finally managed to croak.

He continued. "It's bright red."

"Anything else?"

"Excuse me, I don't mean to interrupt but—"

"Yeah, below it are the words, 'WARNING: HULL PENETRATION.'"

"*Hull Penetration?!*" Wall Street cried. She spun around to me. "Wally, did you hear that?"

I nodded and pointed. "That's what I've been trying to tell you."

She leaned past me to look out the window. "What? Where?"

"There, on the outside of the submarine."

At last she saw it. Now it was her turn to try and talk. "It's . . . ," she swallowed hard.

I nodded. "Yup."

We watched in horrified silence. It was exactly what Opera's warning light showed—the clear, pinkish liquid that had dissolved the potato chip was now dissolving the outside of our minisubmarine!

* * * * *

Again, I'll save you all the embarrassing screaming and hysterical begging for God to save our lives. Let's just say that as much as we enjoyed our little visit to Digestiveland, it was best to be moving on—*as fast as we could!*

But how?

"Guys! . . ." Opera was on the screen again, trying to get our attention. "Guys! GUYS!"

He definitely got our attention that time. And just as soon as our ears quit ringing, we'd be able to hear what he had to say.

"There's some sort of video readout on the screen beside the body diagram."

"Video readout?" I asked. "What's it say?"

"I dunno . . . looks like it explains all about the stomach and intestines and stuff."

"Take a closer look," Wall Street said. "If it's about the digestive system, maybe it will tell us something."

"Let's see, um . . . it says the digestion of food takes several steps. The first step is to chew it up in the mouth and swallow it."

"I think we've already passed that," Wall Street sighed.

I nodded. "We may have missed the chewing, but we definitely got to the swallowing."

Opera continued reading. "After that, it slides down something called the *esophagus* and into the stomach."

"And that's where we are now?" I asked.

"I think so."

"But why's this liquid stuff dissolving everything?" Wall Street asked.

"Hang on, I'm checking . . ."

As Opera read, Wall Street and I looked out the window to the surface of the submarine. It was definitely getting softer and gooier by the second.

"Hurry," Wall Street called. "We don't have much time."

"Ah, here we go. The liquid is called *gastric juice*. It's made up of several enzymes called *pepsin* as well as *hydrochloric acid*."

"*Acid?*" I cried.

Wall Street gasped. "That's why it's dissolving the submarine!"

"We got to get out of here!" I shouted. "Opera, does it say how we can get out?"

"Don't think so. It says some food stays in the stomach for up to five hours!"

"Five hours?" Wall Street cried. "We'll be goners for sure."

"Wait a minute," Opera said. "That's for big pieces of food. It says liquids and small pieces of food pass through the stomach almost immediately."

I looked back out the window. "Unfortunately that's not us. It doesn't look like this submarine is going anywhere."

"That's 'cause it's too big," Wall Street said. "But if it was just us . . . if we were out there on our own, I bet we'd be small enough to get out of here fast."

I gave her a look. "Out there? Without the submarine?"

She nodded.

"You want us to swim out there on our own?"

She motioned toward the back wall. "We've got those diving suits back there."

I glanced to them. "Yeah, but—"

"And ever since we dove for that treasure in Mexico, we know how to scuba dive."

"Yeah, but—"

"And the rubber wet suits will protect our skin from the acid . . ."

"Yeah, but—"

"And if we don't get out of here soon, the hull's going to collapse and we're both going to die!"

I opened my mouth and gave it one last try, but apparently I'd run out of "Yeah, buts."

Don't you hate it when your friends are always right? But she was and there was nothing I could do about it—except let out a long sigh and mumble, "Okay, but if we die, you're going to live to regret it."

* * * * *

Ten minutes later we were suited up. The gear was pretty fancy. Not only were the wet suits and scuba tanks like something from the twenty-third century, but the face mask had a built-in intercom, which was pretty cool, too.

What was not cool was the way I kept stepping on my flippers. No problem—except that stepping on my flippers meant falling on my face. (I guess futuristic equipment can't solve everything.)

"Guys?" It was Opera again, only now we could hear his voice inside our headsets.

"What's up?" Wall Street asked.

"I think you'd better hurry."

"What's the problem?"

"You know that warning light that said, 'Hull Penetration'?"

"Yeah."

"Well, now it's flashing and there's an alarm beeping—"

"No sweat," Wall Street said as she started up the ladder. "We're on our way now."

"Hold it a minute," I said.

"Now what?"

"What are you going to do when you get to the top of that ladder?"

"I'm going to pop the hatch."

"Right, and let a gazillion gallons of that acid splash down on top of us."

"What other choice do we have?" she asked. "It's the only way out."

I shook my head. "There's got to be another way."

"Guys!" Opera warned. "Go! GO!"

It's not that I was chicken or anything like that, it's just that I was . . . well, all right, maybe I was sprouting a few pinfeathers here and there. But I'd rather be a Colonel Sanders special (as long as there was a side order of mashed potatoes and corn-on-the-cob) than have all that liquid acid pounding down on top of me.

I folded my arms and leaned against the submarine's wall, making it clear that I wasn't going anywhere. At least that's what I wanted to make clear. But it would have been a little easier to make it clear if the submarine's wall hadn't already dissolved into something with the consistency of Jell-O.

The good news was that we didn't have to climb out of the hatch's opening. The bad news was that I'd suddenly made my own opening. I quickly fell through the wall with my usual:

"AUGHhhh. . ."

But it wasn't just me. As I fell out, the liquid poured in. And as the liquid poured in, Wall Street was also washed out.

"WALLLLYYYY. . ."

Like it or not, we were both outside the mini-submarine now—or what was left of it. And even as we were swirled around, I could see the hull dissolving and breaking up in a Titanic kind of way.

Now the only thing between us and the stomach's gastric juices were our rubber wet suits. I threw a look to Wall Street. Like me, she was doing her best to swim, but we were both caught in a pretty fierce current—a current that was growing stronger by the second.

Off to my right, I spotted a pinkish wall with hundreds of things, almost like arms or giant fingers, sticking out of it. They were waving back and forth. And directly behind them, on the other side of the wall, were what looked like huge rivers. But these rivers weren't blue. They were red.

"Opera!" I shouted into my intercom. "Where are we now?"

"You've left the submarine!" he cried. "There are a couple of new blips on the screen. It must be you guys."

"But where are we?" I shouted.

"Hang on . . ."

I waited as the current tumbled and tossed us, pulling us closer and closer to the waving arms.

Opera came back on. "Wally?"

"Present."

"It looks like you two are now in the small intestines."

"Small intestines!" Wall Street shouted. "What happens there?"

"Let me see. . . . Ah, here we go. It says: 'The small intestines are where the nutrients are trapped by millions of tiny, fingerlike structures called *villi.*'"

"I see them!" Wall Street cried as she looked toward the arms. "I see the villi!"

Opera continued reading: "The villi trap the food

molecules until they are absorbed through the intestinal walls and into the bloodstream."

"That's wonderful," I shouted. "But what about us? What's going to happen to us?"

"Wally?" Wall Street called.

I paid no attention. "I appreciate the biology lesson, Opera, but—"

"Wally?"

". . . what's it say about—"

"WALLY!"

I turned to her. "What?"

"I think *we* are those molecules."

"What's that supposed to mean?"

She turned back to the wall of arms. She was nearly in them. "It means you and I are small enough to be absorbed through this wall and into the blood—"

But she never finished the sentence. Suddenly, she was caught by one of the arms and—

"WALLY! . . ."

it immediately pulled her in.

"HELP ME! WALLY, IT'S GOT ME!"

I watched in horror. Not only did the arms pull her tight against the wall, but she immediately began to be sucked through it. She was being sucked right through the wall and into the other side! Right into one of those raging red rivers!

"WALLYYY!"

I knew it was time to be the hero. I knew it was time to forget all my past mistakes, step up to the plate, and save my friend's life. And I would have, too, if it wasn't for—

"Uh-oh . . ." Suddenly another arm snagged my own body and started pulling me in. I struggled to get free, but it did no good. Soon I was pinned against the wall. Sooner still, I was getting sucked through that wall! It was a terrible sensation— words could never describe . . . except I suddenly had greater sympathy for milkshakes being drunk through straws.

But this was no time for sympathy. This was a time for action. A time to fight, a time to muster up all my manliness and . . . scream my head off:

"AUGH!!"

I broke through to the other side of the wall. Suddenly, I was in the middle of a raging red river. Suddenly, I was racing through it, completely out of control!

Chapter 4

A Little Swim

"Wally!" Opera cried. "Wally, what's happening?"

"I'm in some sort of river!" I shouted. "It's all around me, like I'm in a giant pipe or something."

"It's a *capillary*," Wall Street yelled. "If this is the bloodstream, then this is one of those capillary things we read about in science."

I spotted her. She was swimming just in front of me. "A what-*illary?*" I shouted.

"She said it's a capillary," Opera answered. It was obvious he was looking at the video readout again. "It says here that they're tiny blood vessels that pick up and deliver oxygen from the lungs and nutrients from the intestines."

"That's what we're being treated like," Wall Street exclaimed. "Right now, this body thinks we're nutrients."

"Wonderful," I sighed. "So now what happens?"

Opera continued reading. "The oxygen and

nutrients will be transported in larger and larger vessels until they arrive at whichever body cells need them."

"And then?"

"And then they'll redivide into another bunch of tiny capillaries to give those cells the oxygen and food they need."

"Hold it," I shouted. "I'm not going to be some cell's after school snack."

"I don't think you have any choice in the matter," Opera said.

"Actually," Wall Street called back, "I don't think we have too much to worry about."

"Why not?"

"Remember that clock in the submarine? The one that showed how much time we have left being miniaturized?"

"Yeah?"

"I entered it into my wristwatch. And if it's correct, we only have a few minutes left before the process is reversed."

"You mean before we start growing bigger?"

She gave a nod. "And become too large for any cell to eat."

"If you're talking about this digital clock labeled: 'Total Miniaturization Time,'" Opera said over our headsets, "I've got one right here on my control board."

"What's it read?" Wall Street asked, looking at her watch. "Five minutes and thirty-three seconds?"

"Exactly," Opera answered.

She gave a sigh of relief. "We'll be big before you know it."

I nodded. "I hope you're right." Suddenly I spotted a huge, flying disc coming up from behind me. It was kinda red, and you could almost see through it. "Wall Street!" I shouted, "Wall Street, what's that!?"

She spun around. Even though she was wearing a face mask I could see her eyes widen in fear.

"Opera?" I cried. "What else are in these blood vessels besides us nutrient-types?"

"Hang on, I'll check. Oh, here we go. It says over half of the blood is made up of something called *plasma.*"

I watched as the flattened saucer continued to approach. "What's plasma?"

"About 90 percent of it's just water."

"This ain't water, pal," I said as the red disk began passing over my head.

"Maybe you're seeing a *platelet,*" he offered.

"A what-*let?*"

"They're small round cells that stick to cuts and form scabs to stop us from bleeding to death."

"This thing isn't small. It looks like a giant, jelly-filled doughnut that's flattened in the middle."

"A jelly-filled doughnut?" Opera shouted. The mention of food definitely got his attention.

"Yeah," I said, "and it's red."

"Hang on . . . still checking. It's not a whitish-clear globby thing, is it? 'Cause that would be a *white blood cell.* They attack germs and stuff."

I glanced around and saw a couple of them floating off in the distance, too. "No," I repeated, "this thing is red and looks like a flying saucer."

"Oh, here we go," he said. "I bet it's a *red blood cell.* That's what carries the oxygen from the lungs to the other cells of the body."

"You're becoming a regular biology professor," I quipped.

"Actually, I wouldn't mind it," Opera said. "This stuff is pretty cool."

I watched as the giant cell finished passing over my head. Talk about awesome. Opera definitely had a point. Even though I was majorly frightened, I was also pretty impressed. I mean, it was incredible to see what we're made of—how we're put together. Let's face it, God must have stayed up a few extra nights dreaming up some of this stuff.

"Wally?"

I turned to Wall Street. She was beside me now. Our capillary or vessel or whatever was getting a lot bigger, and we were picking up speed.

"I wonder whose body we're in?" she asked.

I shrugged. "Got me. But I bet it's going to smart when we start growing."

"So what do we do?" she asked. "Just float around and wait 'til that happens?"

"I guess." But even as I said that, I knew things wouldn't be quite that easy. After all, we are talking about one of my adventures, right? So, to take my mind off of any upcoming, non-stop terror waiting to drop into my future, I began to think about the superhero story again. True, I didn't have any keyboard handy, but I figured I could pretty much keep track of the stuff in my head and type it into Ol' Betsy later. So . . .

When we last left Mirror Man he'd just discovered RetroRunt had stopped the earth and started it spinning in the opposite direction. Talk about major whiplash. But, other than visiting chiropractors the rest of his life, there's one other problem our help-lessly handsome hero, knows he is the only one who can save the day. Worse than that, he knows he'll actually have to leave his mirrors to do it.

It's a scary thought, but there's no other solution.

In a burst of courageously courageous courage our gorgeous good guy pulls himself away from the bathroom mirror and races down the hallway. But he only takes a few steps before he begins to sweat and gasp for breath. Already he is worrying if his hair is straight or if his eyebrows have been brushed. But a superhero's gotta do what a super-hero's gotta do.

He staggers to the door and throws it open. Holy heroics! It's worse than he thought. Outside, cars are running back-ward, people are walking in reverse, and some kid is spitting his ice cream back onto his cone. (Don't even ask about that poor guy who's trying to blow his nose!)

"You've got to help us!" a mother cries as she pulls her baby carriage backward past him. "You're our only hope!"

Mirror Man nods, fully understanding their problem. "I fully understand your problem!" (See, I told you.) "But you've got to tell me one thing!"

"What's that?"

"How does my hair look?"

"Perfect!"

With that bit of encouragement, Mirror Man races out onto the street. But where to begin? How to find the world's tiniest villain? It's not that RetroRunt is short (there's nothing wrong with being short as long as your feet reach all the way to the ground). But this guy is also skinny——so skinny that he makes no.2 pencils feel a need to sign up for weight control classes.

No one's sure how RetroRunt got so scrawny. Some say that as a child he drew too many stick figures on his Etch-a-Sketch and just naturally figured he should look that way. Others say he wanted to be a model like all those other skin-and-bone types in the teen magazines. Then there's the popular theory that he drank all those muscle-building milkshakes in a can, but that he opened the cans upside down, which, of course, meant that they had the opposite effect.

Whatever the reason, RetroRunt is small in an *I'm-afraid-to-be-in-the-bathtub-when-it's-draining* kind of way.

But why would the tiny tot want to keep reliving this same day over and

over again, unless.... Suddenly, Mirror
Man snaps his fingers (but not too hard,
less he damage a nail). Of course, today
was RetroRunt's birthday! But why would
the micro-mite want to keep reliving his
birthday?

(Oh, I know what you're thinking—the
more birthdays the guy has, the more
presents he gets. But the same people
would be coming to the same party with
the same presents. Nice try, dear reader,
but it's better to leave the story-
telling to us professional types.)

Desperately our hero searches his mind
(not so tough when it's so tiny). Unfortunately, he still has no clue. (Come to
think of it, neither do I. Hmm...maybe
I need your help after all.)

But Mirror Man is desperate. It's been
almost two minutes since he's seen a
reflection of himself, and he's starting
to get the shakes. Oh sure, he's caught
his reflection while passing store windows as well as vague outlines of himself in mud puddles. Then there's that
unfortunate incident where he began
chasing the pickup with the shiny chrome
bumper—until it suddenly hit its

brakes. (Hey, who needs all those teeth anyway?) Still, those reflections are poor substitutes (not to mention painful ones) for the real thing.

Then, just as he's about to quit, just as he's about to drag himself into the nearest clothing store and get a good three-way reflection of himself in the mirror, he spots a group of kids exiting the movie theater. And there in the lead is (insert that bad guy music again)...RetroRunt.

Summoning his last ounce of strength our hero staggers toward the menacing villian. "RetroRunt," he cries. "RetroRunt!"

Spotting him, RetroRunt immediately reaches down to his Remote Retrobelt, presses a few buttons—

BEEP...BOP...BURP...BELCH!

Suddenly the Earth's retrorockets are fired. And, instantly, the entire planet comes to a screeching halt.

Unfortunately, you can't say the same about the people. Everyone screams as they tumble forward.

But our famous, flea-high foe is far

"Looks like you're in one of the heart chambers," he said. "Something called the *right atrium.* And that must have been the *tricuspid valve* that closed in front of you."

"Great," I sighed. "So now what do we—"

"Hang on," he interrupted, "it's not over yet."

As he spoke the valve began to open again. That was the good news. Unfortunately, there was a little bad news—as the valve opened, the giant chamber around us began to collapse!

"OPERA!"

"It's okay! That's just the *atrium* contracting. It's getting ready to shoot you through the tricuspid valve and into the next chamber, the . . . *right ventricle.*"

Before I could answer, Wall Street and I were quickly squirted through the opening—

"AUGH!"

and into that next chamber.

But the fun and games weren't exactly over. Suddenly, another wall closed in front of us—

THUD!

and suddenly we came to another screeching stop.

"Opera??"

from finished. He hits another set of buttons—

BELCH...BURP...BOP...BEEP!

and everything begins moving in the right direction again. But not for long.

Our hero knows that soon RetroRunt will send things in reverse again. Soon, everyone will have to go back and relive the day again, and again, and again. Kids will have to go to the same day of school, grownups will have to go to the same day of work, and TV viewers will have to watch the same episode of *Happy Days* for the zillionth time (hmm, I guess some things won't be that different after all).

And then, just when it couldn't look any worse (except for that guy who never gets to finish blowing his nose), everything suddenly—

THUD-THUD

The noise was so loud that it jarred me from my story. But it was more than just a noise. It was a vibration. A thundering vibration so powerful I could feel it through my whole body. In fact, everything around me was shaking with it.

THUD-THUD

I threw a look over to Wall Street. She looked as worried as I felt.

"What is it?" she shouted.

I shook my head. "Opera?" I yelled. "Opera, what's happening?!"

"Uh, guys?" he coughed nervously over our headsets. "I think I've got a little bad news."

"What's going on?" Wall Street demanded.

THUD-THUD

"It looks like the two of you—" He coughed again.

"What is it?!" we both shouted.

"You're in a major blood vessel, and you're heading straight for the heart!!"

Chapter

The Heart of the Ma

The pounding grew deafening. And for good re

"Look!" Wall Street pointed. I spun aroun saw a giant red wall closing in front of us, ing our path.

"What's that?" I shouted.

"You guys are there!" Opera yelled. " inside the heart!"

"What about this wall?" I shouted. "Wha supposed to—" But that's all I got out b finally slammed shut with a powerful—

THUD!

Suddenly our raging river had no plac We came to an immediate stop. Now ev was very still and very quiet.

"Opera?" Wall Street whispered thr headset. "What's going on?"

"That's the *semilunar valve!*" he shouted.

"How many valves does this guy's heart have anyway? I'm getting seasick."

Wall Street agreed. "This is worse than riding with my brother when he had his learner's permit!"

"It's not over yet," Opera warned. "This next part might get a little rough!"

"A *little* rough?" I cried. "What do you think it's been the rest of the—"

"WALLY, LOOK OUT!"

I glanced up just as the top of this new chamber came crashing down onto me. But it wasn't only the top of the chamber. It was all of the chamber—from every side. Suddenly, I felt like the ketchup in one of those little packets as it's being stomped by a very big person—or a very large freight train.

We shot out of there faster than a health food addict from a candy store.

"OPERA!"

"Hang on, guys," he yelled, "hang on!"

It was a pretty good piece of advice considering we didn't have anything else better to do. We continued zipping through the vessel so fast that the force pulled my lips back to my ears—which didn't help much in talking:

"Waalll Freeet," I cried. "Whaaar arrrr woooo?"

I tried looking for her, but the force was so strong I couldn't turn my head. All I could do was stare straight ahead at the blur of blood vessel wall racing by. I did notice that my old buddy, Mr. Red Blood Cell, was sailing right along beside me. But, for some reason, I didn't find that a great comfort.

"Man," Opera yelled through the headset, "you guys are really hauling!"

"Mooo kiiidding," I yelled back. "Boooot whaaar's Waalll Freeet?"

"The screen shows a blip right behind you. That's gotta be her. You're in the pulmonary artery, heading toward the lungs."

"Aaand theen whaaat?"

"Let's see . . . Oh, cool. You get to go back to the heart but to the other side."

"Wooondepuul . . ."

"I'll save you the gorey details. Let's just say that after a quick visit to Lungland and a return to Happy Heartville, we were flying in a brand new direction.

"Hey, check it out," Opera shouted. "Looks like you're heading straight for his brain!"

I could only groan. At last we began to slow down. Through the plasma and past another big red blood cell I spotted Wall Street. I fought against the current, slowing myself until she caught up. When I saw her smiling face, I felt a wave of relief wash over me.

Don't get me wrong, we weren't boyfriend or girlfriend or anything like that. It's just that we'd put in a lot of time together and I'd hate to have to explain to her big brother how I lost her. (Sometimes big brothers can be a pain—actually, they can give pain—if they think you've been inconsiderate toward their little sister. And losing her in some guy's blood vessel might be considered just a little on the inconsiderate side.)

"Wow," she grinned. "Is this awesome or what? It's like some incredible dream."

"Actually, I was thinking more like an incredible nightmare."

"Hey . . ." She was already pointing to something else. "Check it out."

I looked back over my shoulder. We were traveling a lot slower now, and the blood vessel we were in was a lot smaller.

"Looks like we're in another one of those capillary thingies," she said. As she spoke, the passageway grew narrower. In fact, the walls were so close that we could actually reach out and touch either side if we had wanted.

If we wanted. But, of course we didn't. Instead, something else caught both of our attentions. Up ahead, my red blood cell buddy was pressing against both sides of the capillary wall. And, as we watched, the most amazing thing began to happen. The bright red color of the cell started to change. It started to grow darker.

"Cool," Wall Street said.

"What's up?" Opera asked from the lab.

I explained to him what was happening, and he quickly searched the files until he found an explanation. "You're watching something called *diffusion*. I bet it looks pretty neat."

"It would look neater if I knew what it was."

"Sorry," he answered. "If that red blood cell is changing color then I bet it's passing oxygen through the capillary wall to a body cell that's breathing it in from the other side."

"Breathing it in?" Wall Street said. "You mean cells breathe?"

"That's right."

"Like people?"

"Sort of. At least that's what it says here. Not only do they breathe in oxygen, but they breathe out *carbon dioxide*," Opera continued to read. "And it's the red blood cells that carry oxygen and carbon dioxide back and forth from the lungs."

I looked on as the red blood cell continued to grow darker and darker brown. "So," I asked, making sure I understood, "this red blood cell guy is actually giving the other cell oxygen through the capillary wall?"

"Kinda like mouth-to-mouth resuscitation?" Wall Street asked.

"Something like that. Only it also sucks out the other cell's carbon dioxide," Opera said.

"Very cool," I said.

"But what about all these sparkling lights?" Wall Street asked.

I looked around. "What lights?"

"There, on the other side of the wall." She pressed her face mask closer to the capillary wall. "What are all those lights shooting back and forth . . . looks like electricity or something."

I swam closer to the wall. It was so thin I could almost see through it. She was right. Ever so faintly I could see sparking and flashing on the other side. I moved closer, cupping my hands around my face mask and pressing it against the wall for a better look. The flashings were like little bolts of lighting. But it wasn't just one bolt. There were hundreds of them flashing everywhere.

"Opera?"

"Checking."

We waited as he continued to search. "Let's see, if you're in the brain looking out at the cells . . . ah, here we go."

"What's up?" I asked.

"You must be watching the cells in the brain communicate with each other."

"No way."

"Yup. It says that brain cells talk back and forth to each other with electricity."

"You mean, we got electricity shooting around inside our brains?" I asked.

"That's what it says. But in very, very small amounts. And when that electricity is firing, that's when the cells are thinking."

"This is incredible," Wall Street said in quiet awe. And she was right, it was incredible. Everywhere we looked lights were flashing.

"This guy must be a regular Einstein," I said.

"Not really. It says that the average brain cell can fire electricity a bunch of times every second."

"Wow," I said. "This has definitely got to be one of God's better inventions."

I don't know how long we floated there staring, but eventually we felt a gentle push. I glanced over and saw that the red blood cell had let go of the capillary wall and was starting to move forward again. So were we.

"Hey Opera?" I called. "Where are we headed now?"

As usual, his mouth was full of food, and it took him a moment to swallow. I sort of wished he was as concerned about us as he was his junk food, but I guess some habits are hard to break. Finally, he answered. "According to this chart, that red blood cell is going back to the heart and lungs to drop off the carbon dioxide it just picked up.

"Been there!" I cried.

"Done that!" Wall Street agreed.

"Yeah," Opera said. "I see your point. If you want, I suppose you can swim back upstream a ways and try out another capillary."

I looked to Wall Street. She shrugged. "As long as we hurry. We start getting big again in two minutes and fifty-two seconds."

I nodded. We pushed off and headed back upstream until we entered into another smaller capillary.

Suddenly, we were surrounded by blinding light. I squinted, trying to make out what was happening, but the capillary was flooded with glaring brightness.

"What is it?" Wall Street shouted. "Where's all that light coming from?"

"Opera!" I yelled. "Where are we?"

"Looks like you've entered this guy's eye. You're in a capillary at the back of his eyeball."

"You're kidding!" I shouted. "And all this light is—"

"It's what he's seeing. It's all coming from the front of his eye."

I turned to Wall Street with amazement. "Is this cool, or what?"

She grinned back. "Maybe cooler than you think."

"What do you mean?"

"If we're in this guy's eyeball, then maybe we can look out of it and see what he's seeing."

"Really?"

She nodded. "And if we see what he's seeing then maybe we'll be able to figure out who he is."

Opera came back on the headset. "She might have a point. If you're at the right place in the back of the eye, you might be able to see through the capillary and see what he's seeing."

Suddenly, Wall Street shouted. "There!" She had pressed her face mask back against the wall. "I see something!"

"What?" I swam over to join her.

"Take a look."

I pressed my mask against the wall and all the glaring light started to come into focus.

"What are you guys seeing?" Opera asked.

"It's hard to tell," I said, squinting. "It's sort of flat and wavy and—

"And yellow," Wall Street added. "Definitely yellow."

Then it disappeared. Just like that. But before

Wall Street or I could comment, another one came into view. By now I was getting used to all the light, and I could make out more detail. "It looks like . . . Wall Street, is that what I think it is?"

She nodded. "It might be. . ."

"Opera?"

"Yeah?"

"It looks like some sort of potato chip is coming toward us."

"No way," he said. Suddenly the chip disappeared.

"Well, it's gone now," I shrugged.

"You sure it was a potato chip?" he asked through another mouthful of food.

"I think so."

"Wait a minute," Wall Street said. "Here comes something else."

We both watched as a round, shiny something came toward us. "What is that?" she asked.

I squinted harder. "I can't tell for sure, but it looks like . . . is that a soda can coming at us?"

"A soda can?" Opera asked. "How weird."

But not as weird as what happened next—because as the can came closer we were able to make out a faint reflection on its shiny surface. In fact, as it was being lifted toward us, we saw what actually looked like a face staring back at us. True, things were kinda blurry, and the entire image was upside down, but it only took a second for us to recognize it.

I wanted to say something, anything . . . but it's hard to talk when your heart has leaped into your throat.

"Hey, guys," Opera asked, "What's going on?"

I threw a look over to Wall Street. She was having the same problem.

"Guys?"

I swallowed hard.

Wall Street swallowed hard.

"Guys, what do you see?"

Finally, at the same time, we answered in hoarse, raspy voices: "We see you!"

Chapter 6
"Growing UP"

Ever notice how good friends sort of pick up each other's habits? Good or bad, we start doing what the other guy does. At least that's how it was between Opera and me. And, being my best friend for just slightly longer than forever, it was only natural for him to give my world famous screaming a shot:

"AUGHHHHHHhhhh . . ."

For the most part, he wasn't bad. In fact, on the McDoogle Panic Scale of one to ten, he was pushing an eleven. Of course he had plenty of reason. How often do you discover your two best friends are floating around your skull? (Talk about getting inside somebody's head.)

The yelling was good. But where my bud really showed his stuff was in all the jumping and bouncing around he was doing. Of course, I would have enjoyed it a bit more if I wasn't also getting bounced around.

"Op-er-er-er-a!" I cried. Suddenly, I was slammed against one side of the capillary wall.

"Someb-b-b-body stop-p-p-p him!" Wall Street screamed until she was suddenly slammed against the other side.

But Opera was a little too busy with his panic attack to pay us much attention. So there we were getting tossed up and down and back and forth. And just when we were getting used to that, it was down and up and forth and back. Still, despite all the fun and games, I knew something was missing. I mean for an official McDoogle Mishap we needed a little something else. We needed that one, extra catastrophe, that one little—

BEEP BEEP BEEP BEEP

I spun to Wall Street who was flying past me on her way into the opposite wall. "What is that?" I cried.

"That's my watch alarm!" she yelled as

BOING!

she bounced off the wall and flew toward me.

Of course, I was busy doing the same thing off of the opposite wall.

BOING!

And when we passed each other again in the middle, I shouted: "What's it mean?"

BOING!

She bounced.
BOING!

I bounced.
"I set it to go off when that miniaturization clock ran out of time. It means we're starting to get bigger!"
"That's just great!" I shouted.

BOING!
BOING!

"Maybe," she cried as she came back toward me.
"What do you mean 'maybe'?" I shouted. Only this time I slightly changed course and:

K-BAMB!
"OAFF!"

The good news was we'd stopped bouncing back and forth off the walls. The bad news was we broke more than our share of bones when we slammed into each other. Still, a few broken body parts seemed a minor price to pay to stop our human pinball imitation.

"Opera!" I shouted. "Opera!"

But he still wasn't listening.

"Come on," Wall Street yelled as she kicked and paddled her way back toward the eyeball. "Let's see what he's doing."

I followed. We were still getting bounced around pretty good, but I managed to hang on and press my face mask against the wall to take a look. To my surprise, there was Opera, staring straight back at me. He still had his headset on so I knew he'd be able to hear. It was just a matter of waiting until he was done with his little panic attack.

"Guys!" he shouted. "Guys, are you still there? I'm in the restroom now. I'm looking into a mirror. Guys! Wall Street? Are you there? Wally? Wall Street!"

He finally took a breath, which allowed me to finally squeeze in a word. "Opera, we're still here! We haven't gone anywhere!"

"How'd you do it?" he cried. "How did you get inside of me?"

"You must have swallowed us," Wall Street said.

"No way," he argued. "The only thing I've eaten are these chips." He showed us his fifteenth bag of Chippy Chipper Potato Chips. "And this soda." He held up the can.

Suddenly, I had this sinking feeling in my gut. "Opera?" I shouted. "Where did you get that can of pop?"

"I found it on the floor where the minisubmarine was. It was still cold, and no one was drinking it, so—"

"Actually," I cleared my throat. "I'm afraid someone *was* drinking it."

"Who?"

"Me."

"You?"

"When I climbed up into the submarine, I set that can down on the platform below it."

Wall Street let out a loud groan. "Are you telling me that when we got miniaturized . . . we dropped right into your soda pop can?"

I nodded feeling even sicker. "That would explain all that bubbly liquid we saw."

She dully added, "And the round metal wall that surrounded us."

Opera took it from there. "So when I picked up that can and drank it . . ."

"You drank us," I said.

There was a moment of silence. I continued looking out the capillary wall as Opera leaned closer to the mirror. Now we were eyeball to eyeball.

"How come I can't see you?" he asked. "If you're really in there, how come I don't see you?"

"Because, we're still inside a blood vessel," I explained. "Besides, we're too small."

"Not for long," Wall Street said.

I turned to her and she motioned to her wristwatch. "The miniaturization is wearing off, remember?"

"So we're getting bigger?"

She nodded. "Take a look around you. See how small the capillary looks now."

I glanced around. She was right.

"Wait a minute!" Opera interrupted. It sounded like he was getting worked up again. "If you're starting to grow bigger and if you're still inside of me . . ." He came to a stop.

I watched as his eyes widened in horror. Suddenly, I realized what he realized. I threw a look over to Wall Street. She realized it, too. Now, all three of us knew what would happen to Opera if we kept growing inside of him. And with that bit of understanding, we looked at each other and did the only thing we could do. This time in three part harmony:

"AUGH!!!!!!!!!!!!!!!!!!!"

After we finished our little trio, Opera decided to go solo. "What do I do?? What do I do?! What do I do!?"

The lyrics were a little monotonous so I shouted, "There's not much you can do! We're the ones who have to get out of here!"

"But how?!" he cried.

"Don't worry," I yelled, "we'll think of something. The important thing is that you don't panic." But even as I shouted these words my head scraped against the top of the capillary.

So did Wall Street's.

We were growing—and FAST!

"We've got to get out of these little vessels," I shouted. "We've got to get into some bigger ones."

Wall Street agreed. We pushed off and started swimming for all we were worth. We had to get out of there, and we had to get out of there now.

"Opera," I called. "You gotta get help. You gotta find Mr. Pocket Protector!"

Opera yelled back. "Everyone's gone! They all left!"

"Keep trying," I shouted. "We've got to get some help. Somebody's got to—"

"WALLY!"

It was Wall Street. I spun around and spotted her several feet behind me. She was no longer swimming. Instead, she was kicking and fighting off one of the white blood cell thingies as it wrapped itself around her leg.

"It's got me!" she cried. "It won't let me go!"

I quickly swam back to her. Even as I approached the thing was covering more and more of her leg.

"What's happening?" Opera yelled.

"One of the white blood cells grabbed Wall Street."

"Help me!" she screamed. "Help me!"

I arrived at her side. By now it had swallowed her whole leg and was moving up to her waist.

"Opera, get back to the monitors!" I shouted. "Tell us what's going on!"

"Wally, get it off me! Get it off me!"

I grabbed the clear goop, but the cell was like jelly, impossible to get a good grip on. And the more I tried pulling and scraping it away, the more goop swarmed back in its place.

"Opera!"

"I'm checking, I'm checking!"

It was surrounding her stomach now. Like a giant, hungry jellyfish, it was slowly but surely swallowing her whole.

"Get it off me!" she gasped. "Get it off me!"

"Opera!"

"Let's see . . . white blood cells, white blood cells. Here we go."

"Hurry!" she coughed. It had moved up her chest and was starting to cut off her breathing.

Opera continued reading. "It says there are five types of white blood cells: *Lymphocytes, Antigen—presenting Cells, T Cells—*"

"Not now," I shouted. "Just tell me what's going on. Why's this thing attacking Wall Street?"

"Maybe you've made it mad!"

"We haven't done a thing," I shouted. "We're doing exactly what we've done since we got in here."

"Except . . ." Wall Street coughed, fighting for air. "Except we're growing."

Of course, she was right. We were growing. In fact, the only reason the cell hadn't completely swallowed her was she was growing faster than it could keep up.

"I've got it!" Opera shouted.

"What?" I cried.

"The thing is attacking her because it thinks she's an intruder. That's what white blood cells do—they seek and destroy bacteria, viruses, and other junk that attack the body."

"But we're not attacking your body!" I yelled.

"I know it and you know it . . . but that white blood cell doesn't. Right now, it thinks she's the enemy, and it's trying to eat her."

"Eat me!" Wall Street screamed.

"That's what they do."

"But why now?" I shouted. "Why's it attacking now?"

"Because I'm bigger," Wall Street repeated as she gasped for breath. "Before, it thought I was a nutrient . . . but now I'm big enough for it to see me as a threat."

"But why you?" I demanded.

"It's not just me."

"What?"

"Look at your leg."

I glanced down to see another white blood cell arrive. It grabbed my leg, but before I could peel it off, another one grabbed my arm! And then my other arm. Suddenly it had turned into a major party.

And by the looks of things, Wall Street and I were the only refreshments.

Chapter 7

Swim!!!

The good news was we were growing faster than the white blood cells could swallow us. The bad news was they were sending in more recruits.

"Look!" Wall Street cried. "Over there!"

I twirled around to see another dozen of their buddies barreling down the blood vessel directly at us. "What do we do?" I shouted.

"Go back to Plan A!"

"Plan A? I'm sorry, I forgot what—"

"Swim!" she yelled. "Swim like you never swam before."

I suppose we could have discussed the other options, but I didn't particularly want to stay around and talk. I mean it's one thing to have a few cells that we were outgrowing hang onto us. It was quite another to be smothered to death by a whole herd of them.

We pushed off and began swimming for all we

were worth. Even though we made pretty good progress, the fresh recruits racing toward us quickly closed in.

"Opera!" I shouted. "Help us! Tell us what we can do!"

"There's nothing you can do."

"What??"

"Those white cells are built to kill intruders. They're impossible to stop."

"Opera!"

"I'm serious. Without special drugs or treatment from the outside, there's no way you can stop them!"

"This is great," I cried, "just great."

"Actually it is great, I mean when you stop to think about it. They're really pretty cool inventions."

I'm sure he had a point, but at the moment I had a few other things on my mind—like surviving. I looked back over my shoulder. The cells were definitely gaining on us. I turned to Wall Street who was swimming beside me.

"You mentioned Plan A," I gasped between swim strokes. (Don't worry, I gasp when I do anything physical, particularly if it resembles exercise. It's not that I'm out of shape. In fact, I'm planning to try out for the Olympics—just as soon as they have an event for Channel Surfing.) "What about Plan B!" I cried. "Or Plan C?"

"There is no Plan C," she said.

"Then what about Plan B?"

"You don't want to know."

"Sure I do."

"No, you don't!"

I glanced over my shoulder. They'd almost reached us. "What is Plan B?" I cried. "Tell me about Plan B!"

"Plan B is to quit swimming and be eaten."

I swam harder.

"Guys!" It was Opera again. "My chart shows you're coming up to another large blood vessel on the right."

I looked ahead and spotted another vessel emptying into ours. "I see it!" I shouted.

"Good. Maybe you can duck in there and lose them."

"Don't be ridiculous," I cried.

"No," Wall Street said. "He might have a point. If we can squeeze in there, and if we can somehow block off the opening, they might not be able to get to us."

"What about the other side?" I argued. "New ones will come at us from the other side."

"We can block it off, too," she said.

It sounded pretty lame, but I suppose it was better than the plan I'd dreamed up (which involved breaking into tears and crying for my mommy). "Okay," I shouted. "Let's do it!"

We swam toward the other vessel. As we approached the opening, we reached out and grabbed it. The thing was slipperier than slug slime, but we hung on.

Wall Street was the first to begin pulling herself inside. It was obvious that we were still growing, and even as she climbed into the opening it seemed to be getting smaller and smaller.

I glanced over my shoulder. "Hurry," I shouted. "They're practically here!"

At last she was inside.

Now it was my turn. I grabbed the wall and tried to pull myself in. I might have made it if I wasn't lacking this thing called "coordination." (Okay, I lied about the Olympics—the truth is I sprain my thumb just pressing those channel selector buttons.) Anyway, it was becoming obvious I was going to fail in a major, I-think-I'm-going-to-die kind of way, so I resorted to the only other thing I knew:

"HELP ME!" I begged. "HELP ME! HELP ME! HELP ME!"

I was grateful to see Wall Street reaching out to me. I wasn't grateful to see the white cell gang arrive and start wrapping themselves around my legs. Nor was I thrilled when they started pulling me away. I was losing my grip, unable to hang on, about to be swept off to some white cell dinner with me as the main course. Then, at the last second, Wall Street lunged forward and grabbed my wrist.

Now, before you get any ideas, let me just say that normally I'm not crazy about holding a girl's hand. But since I have this thing about living, I decided to make an exception. I hung on to her as she dug her feet into her vessel's wall and began pulling me in.

There wasn't much I could do to help. The growing mass of cells around my legs made it nearly impossible to move. But Wall Street would not give up. She groaned and tugged and pulled. And when she got tired of that, she pulled and tugged and groaned . . . until finally my head was up and inside the other vessel. Next came my chest, then my stomach . . . until everything but my legs were inside. I turned around and quickly drew them in, managing to scrape off most of my uninvited dinner guests.

But the fun and games weren't quite over. The current rushing inside our new vessel was pretty strong. We had to wedge ourselves in tightly against its walls. Then there were all those frustrated white cells who were trying to slip in through the opening after me.

"Here!" Wall Street shouted. She was removing her swim fins. "Take my flippers and shove them into that opening to block them."

We (and all of our gear) were growing large enough to where that just might work. I grabbed one of her fins and turned toward the opening. A few cells were nearly inside. But, using the fin, I shoved and pushed the jellylike things until I squished them back out.

Wall Street was already handing me her other fin. I grabbed it and quickly wedged both of them into the opening until I created a type of flipper wall. Of course the white cells kept trying to push in, but between the outgoing current and my flipper roadblock they didn't have a chance.

Unfortunately, there was the other side.

"Say, Wally . . ."

I turned to see a brand new batch of cells racing toward us from the other end of the vessel.

"Here." I ripped off my fins and passed them to Wall Street. She took them and quickly built another flipper wall on her side.

At last we were sealed in nice and safe. A little snug, but definitely safe. And it was great to finally catch our breath.

Unfortunately, there was one little problem.

"Guys . . ." It was Opera again. "Guys, what are you doing? Guys, something's wrong."

"It's okay," I said. "We're okay, we're just resting."

"It's not you," he answered. "It's me."

"What do you mean?"

"I'm getting . . . it's like I'm getting all dizzy and . . . and part of my body is getting numb."

Wall Street and I exchanged looks.

"Are you sure?" I asked.

"Sure I'm sure. My right hand and arm . . . even part of my right leg is losing feeling."

"Opera!" Wall Street sounded pretty concerned. "Opera, can you get back to the control station and see what that readout says?"

"I'mm thitting thar . . . noowww . . ."

She frowned. "Say again?"

"I thad I'mm awready thitting . . ." he coughed.

She spun back to me. "His speech . . . something's happening to his speech!"

"Opera?"

"Thomming ith tarriply wong. I think I'm gooing to . . . Guyths, I think I'm gooing to pathh ouuu . . ." He never finished the sentence. Instead, he let out a quiet groan followed by a tremendous crash that Wall Street and I felt from inside.

"Opera?" I shouted. "Opera, can you hear me?!"

There was no answer.

"Opera!" Wall Street cried. "Opera, are you there? Opera!"

"It's no good," I said. "He must have passed out."

"That's what he was trying to say," Wall Street agreed. "He was dizzy and starting to pass out."

I frowned. "But why? What did we do? Could it be all the excitement?"

She shook her head. "That wouldn't explain why part of his body went numb."

"Wait a minute!" I cried. "Last year! My grandpa had a stroke!"

"So?"

"So those same sort of things happened to him. He lost feeling in part of his body, he got all dizzy, and then he passed out."

"What about his speech?"

"Yes," I nodded, getting more and more concerned. "It was the same thing. In fact, he's still trying to learn to talk again."

Wall Street shook her head. "That can't be right. Strokes are for old people. That's when their blood vessels get all clogged up with fat and junk and—"

"—and miniaturized friends stopping them up with swimming gear?"

She came to a stop. "You don't think we're . . ."

We looked over to our flippers. It was true. As far as stopping up the blood vessel, we'd done a pretty impressive job. And as far as giving our friend a stroke, we were probably doing that, too!

"We've got to get out of here," she said. "We've got to unplug this blood vessel!"

"What about our buddies?" I motioned toward

the white blood cells that had crowded against both ends of our little hideaway. "If we step out of here, they'll get us for sure."

"What other choice do we have?" she asked.

Of course, she was right.

"If we leave now, if we unclog this vessel he'll recover. But if we stay here too long . . ."

I finished the sentence for her. "Opera may *never* recover."

"Or he may die."

Everything grew very quiet. Neither one of us spoke. We knew that if we went back out into that other vessel, we'd be eaten by those white blood cells. But if we stayed here and continued to grow, we'd wind up paralyzing or even killing our friend. Then all three of us would be dead.

I couldn't help thinking back on all our adventures together. How we first met at Camp Whacko . . . how we formed Dork-oids Anonymous . . . how we'd done everything from flying balloons to starring in movies, dodging secret agents, attacking fleas, charging bulls, and every other dangerous thing hazardous to your health.

And now, suddenly, I could be ending his life?

"So which is it?" Wall Street asked. "If we stay here, he'll probably die."

"And if we step out there . . ."

She finished my sentence, "We'll die."

I looked back down to the white blood cells hungrily pushing against the fins trying to get us. Finally, I spoke. "I say we make a run for it."

Wall Street stared at the bulging fins. "Our chances are pretty slim."

"At least we'd have some, which is more than Opera would have if we stay."

"But where will we go?" Wall Street asked. "There's got to be some way out."

We both sat a moment, thinking.

"Wally?"

I turned to her.

"Remember that red blood cell we followed around?"

"Yeah."

"Opera said it was going back to the lungs, right?"

"I think so. Why?"

"What if we were to do that?" she asked. "What if we were to make a run for it and try to get to the lungs before these cells get us?"

"What good would that do?"

"Maybe we could work our way out of the blood vessel. You know, like the oxygen and carbon dioxide do."

"And then what?" I asked.

"And then . . . maybe we could somehow crawl out of the lungs. You know, up his windpipe or something like that."

"Sounds way too risky," I said.

She agreed. "You're right, but . . ."

I turned back to her, knowing her thoughts. "But it's Opera's only chance."

She nodded. So did I.

"All right," I said. "Let's do it."

Without a word she reached for her swim fins. I did the same with mine.

"You ready?" she asked.

I nodded. "On my count. One . . ."

I tightened my grip, getting ready to yank out the flippers and swim like crazy.

"Two . . ."

My entire body tightened, getting ready to spring.

"THREE!"

Chapter 8

Just Like Old Slimes

I yanked the flippers out of the opening, and the white cells came pouring in. I ducked my head and began pushing my way through the slimy things. It was majorly gross and gooey (unless you like swimming in jelly—which I'm not crazy about, but, hey, everyone has a favorite pastime).

Fortunately, I was still wearing my mask, which kept the little critters off my face and hair. Unfortunately, I was still the same coordinationally challenged person. This meant I didn't completely push off in the direction I wanted to go . . .

Which meant I didn't completely go the direction I wanted to go . . .

Which meant I kinda tripped, stumbled, and went in no direction at all.

"Wally, quit fooling around!"

I glanced up and saw Wall Street following in

my footsteps . . . (except for the part where she did everything right). Like me, she had broken through the wall of gooey cells and entered the vessel. But, unlike me, she shot down that vessel straight as an arrow. She was already in the current and quickly disappearing out of sight.

"Hurry!" she cried, just before vanishing. "Hurry!"

I figured it wouldn't hurt to take her advice (especially since all the white blood cells had decided I was the site for their next convention). I pushed off again, this time going straighter and stronger.

The good news was I caught the main current and started racing through the blood vessel. The bad news was all my white blood cell buds tried to hitch a free ride. They would have succeeded, too, if it wasn't for one little

K-BAMB!

problem. I'd slammed into the vessel wall. I glanced around trying to figure out what was going on. I mean I was heading straight and everything, but

K-BAMB!

the vessel wasn't. In fact it had more twists and

kinks than Mom's hair after Aunt Zelda tried to give her a home perm.

K-BAMB!

Let's face it, it was hard enough for me to swim— and now I was expected to swim *and* steer? (The fact that I was getting bigger and the walls were getting closer didn't make the job any easier.) Luckily though,

K-BAMB!

with every collision, I knocked off a couple of hundred of those white cell critters. At this rate,

K-BAMB!

they'd soon be forgotten memories. Which, if I wasn't careful,

K-BAMB!

so would I.

But, just as I was getting tired of the same boring sound effect (not to mention the same bruised and broken body parts) another sound began:

THUD-THUD

Actually it wasn't all that new. I recognized it immediately and shouted through the headset, "Wall Street! Wall Street, can you hear me?"

"Loud and clear," she answered.

THUD-THUD

"Is that what I think it is?"

"If you're thinking it's the heart, you're thinking right."

"We've got to go through that again?"

"It's the only way back to the lungs. But don't worry," she shouted. "I just went through it. Now that we're bigger, it's a lot easier."

Of course, Wall Street's version of a lot easier wasn't exactly the same as mine. I was about to point this out to her when—

THUD-THUD

I saw it. Up ahead. A small porthole that opened and closed with each

THUD-THUD!

I knew it was one of those valve thingies—like the ones we'd slipped through earlier.

THUD-THUD

Only, now that I was bigger, I wasn't so sure
that "slipping through" would be all that simple.
True, I still had more than enough room, but

THUD-THUD

more than enough room isn't always enough
when dealing with my incredible athletic skills.
Still, it wasn't like I had a lot of choice in the
matter since

THUD-THUD

the current was carrying me directly toward it.
   So after a short prayer, where I carefully pointed
out what a great guy I'd been lately, I stretched out
my body, closed my eyes, and sped toward the valve.

THUD-THUD

The sound exploded in my ears. It grew louder
and louder and . . .

THUD-THUD

louder some more. I was nearly there. For the
briefest moment, I actually thought I might
make it until, suddenly—

THUD "OUCH!"

reality set in. This reality had to do with getting my air tank hung up in the valve, which meant

THUD "OUCH!"

I was hung up on the valve, which meant every time it closed shut

THUD "OUCH!"

it closed shut on me. So, with nothing to do but feel myself being pounded into a combo platter for The House of Pancakes, I decided to add some words to all that heart-pounding rhythm. The lyrics were simple and went something like this:

"WALL STREEEET!!!"

A moment later she swam back to my side. I couldn't tell if she was interested in saving my life or stopping my singing. Probably both. She grabbed my head and started pulling.

"Ow!"

She pulled harder.

"OWW!"

Not much was happening—although I did notice
my neck getting longer.

"OWWWW!"

I was just about to stop her (and suggest she
never become a chiropractor), when she gave one
last tug, and I popped out of the valve like a cork
from a bottle.

I have to admit it was getting a little embarrassing always having my life saved by a girl. But
considering my other option (not having my life
saved at all), I figured I'd go ahead and let her
have her fun. After all, everybody needs a hobby.

As the two of us raced down the blood vessel, I
noticed we were continuing to grow and the vessel was continuing to shrink. "We better hurry," I
shouted. "If we don't get out of here soon, who
knows what we'll do to Opera."

"Did somebody mention my name?"

My heart leaped to my throat. It was my buddy!
He was back. "Opera!" I cried. "Are you all right?!"

"Yeah," he mumbled. "Just a little woozy. What
happened? Where are you guys?"

"We're heading for your lungs," Wall Street said.
"We're going to try and get out through them."

"How? You're still in my bloodstream."

"It's going to be tricky, but I think the only way

to get out is to cut a hole in one of these blood vessels and crawl out into your lungs."

"Cut a hole!"

"It won't be big," she said, "just enough for us to squeeze through."

"There's got to be another way!" he cried.

"We're open to suggestions," I said.

"Hang on, let me get back to the control board," he said. We waited as he moved into place. "All right, I'm here."

"What do you see?" Wall Street asked.

"You've left the heart, and you're in one of my *pulmonary arteries*."

"One of your what?" I asked.

"They're the blood vessels that go back to the lungs. They branch off and get smaller and smaller until they turn into those little capillaries again."

"Only this time," Wall Street asked, "don't the red blood cells breathe *out* the carbon dioxide and breathe *in* the oxygen?"

"Exactly," Opera said. "And once they've done that, they'll head back to my heart and then go out to my body again."

I groaned. "No offense, Big Guy, but one trip through your body is enough."

"He's right," Wall Street agreed. "We've got to get out, and it's got to be now."

For a moment, Opera gave no answer. Finally,

he spoke. "You really think cutting a hole in my artery is the only way out?"

"We'll get into the smallest capillary we can," Wall Street said. "That way there shouldn't be too much bleeding."

"Then we'll crawl through the hole, into your lungs, up your windpipe, and out your mouth," I said.

"But once you cut me, how will I stop bleeding?"

Wall Street and I exchanged glances. He had a point.

"Wait a minute," Opera said. "Hang on, let me check something."

I glanced down at my body. The white blood cells had found us again and were starting to cover us. Only now we were so big and they were so small, it didn't make much difference—at least for the time being.

Finally, Opera came back on line. "Guys? Remember way back when you first got into my bloodstream—remember those *platelet* things that I said were in it?"

"Yeah," I answered. "Sort of."

"It says here that when there's a cut in the body and when those platelets are exposed to air . . . it says that they form a seal over the opening to stop the bleeding."

"No way," I said.

"That's what it says. It says that's what makes scabs . . . when they build up and cover the wound."

Wall Street whistled softly. "Talk about cool."

I couldn't help agreeing. "God didn't miss a trick."

Wall Street nodded. "So if we make a cut, it should heal."

"As long as you don't make it too big," Opera cautioned.

I nodded. "But where do you think we should make it?"

"According to this chart," Opera said, "you're already in my lungs. So find the smallest capillary you can and go for it."

I looked over to Wall Street who was already nodding. Without a word, we began searching for the right capillary—something big enough for us to fit in, but small enough so it would quickly heal.

And there it was, dead ahead.

I motioned to Wall Street who saw it, too. We swam over to the opening and began wedging ourselves inside. It was a tight fit, almost as tight as Dad squeezing into those jeans he's way too big for (and keeps blaming the dryer for shrinking). Still, it was something we had to do.

Finally, when we could go no further, Wall Street turned to me and asked, "Have you got a knife?"

I shook my head. "I try to avoid carrying sharp objects."

"And the world's a safer place because of it."

"So what do we use?" I asked.

She began digging into her wet suit.

"Wall Street?"

"I'm getting my fingernail file."

"Your fingernail file?!"

"I never leave home without it."

I could only shrug. Girls, go figure.

Once she found it, she handed it over to me until she caught herself. "Wait a minute. I should probably do this, huh?"

"Only if we want to succeed," I suggested. Then, clearing my throat, I called out to Opera. "We're all set. Are you ready, Big Guy?"

His answer was a little shaky. "You sure this is the only way?"

"Looks like it," Wall Street answered.

He coughed slightly. "Well, all right . . . let's get it over with."

Wall Street looked to me, and I nodded. She raised the file high over her head, hesitated for the briefest second, and then plunged it deep into my best friend's body.

Chapter 9

Break Out!

"Okay guys," Opera called. "Any time. Guys? Oh, guys?"

By the sound of it, he hadn't felt a thing.

"Hey, guys? What are you doing in there? Hello?"

I suppose I should have been polite and answered, but it's hard remembering your manners when you're busy getting killed.

You see, at first everything had gone just fine. Wall Street had stabbed the fingernail file into Opera's blood vessel nice and deep. She'd even managed to pull the file down and make a big enough slit for us to crawl through. Unfortunately, crawling through that slit wouldn't be an option. It's hard to crawl through any slit when you're being swept through it by a raging current.

"AUGHhhh. . ."

The little blood flood shoved us through the hole and out into the lung faster than a kid can hide steamed broccoli in his dinner napkin. I was spun and tumbled like one of those socks Mom keeps losing in the dryer. For a moment I was literally clueless about which end was up (I know, I know, so what else is new). It wasn't until I passed through a forest of midget trees and grabbed hold of one that I finally came to a stop.

Midget trees?!

Well, I guess it really wasn't a tree. I mean when I looked up I couldn't see any leaves or branches or anything. It was just a black, ten-foot pole that waved back and forth like the million other ten-foot poles surrounding it.

Whatever it was, tree or pole, it didn't matter. I just hung on and waited as the river of blood quickly shrunk, then dried up all together.

I tell you it was definitely weird to feel dry ground under my feet again. And I was more than a little glad to finally be able to stand. The surface was soft and spongy, but it definitely held my weight.

Then there was the wind. We're not talking a gentle breeze here. No, this was definitely hurricane stuff. But, as soon as I braced myself against it coming from one direction, it changed and came from the opposite direction. Then it changed to the first direction again. Then to the opposite. Talk about confusing. It took a while before I finally figured out the reason:

If I was in the lungs, then this was Opera breathing . . . in and then out, in and then out.

Trying to stand against the wind was tough, but you didn't hear me complain. No, sir. Whatever direction he breathed, it meant air . . . which meant I could breathe without the scuba tanks . . . which meant I could finally pull off my face mask and gulp in the fresh air.

It was wonderful. Marvelous . . . well, except for the smell of slightly stale potato chips.

I turned back to the artery I'd just come from. Although there were plenty of those waving poles blocking my view, I could still catch a glimpse of the hole Wall Street had cut—at least what was left of it. Talk about amazing. Those platelet thingies had attached themselves to the opening and were already sealing it up.

Incredible.

And then, ever so faintly, over the howling wind, I heard Wall Street. "Wally . . . help me . . . Wally . . ."

But I didn't hear her over the radio headset. This time it was out in the open. I spun around, looking all directions.

"Wall Street!" I shouted. "Where are you?"

"Help me . . ."

And then I spotted something off in the distance.

A clear, liquid wall. A wall of thick goo that rose up through the poles and flowed over the top of them like a stream. A slow moving wall of liquid that was being pushed forward by the waving poles. And there, on top of the thick, gooey stream, was Wall Street!

"Wally . . ." she gasped. "It's got me stuck. I can't move!"

Without thinking, I leaped into action (which, of course, meant crashing into a couple of dozen of those pole things along the way). But that was my friend up there, and somebody had to help her—even if that somebody had to be me.

"Opera," I shouted over the radio as I continued running (and crashing). "Opera, are you there?"

"Where have you guys been?" he asked.

"It doesn't matter," I shouted. "Where are we now? And what's with all these waving poles and this gooey stream?"

"Gooey stream? Waving poles?"

"Yeah, they're long and tall and keep waving back and forth."

"Hang on, I'll check . . ."

When I finally arrived at the stream, it was pretty weird to look up and see the wall flowing past me. The stuff was so thick and sticky it wouldn't spread out. And there, trapped on top of the stream, like a fly to flypaper, was Wall Street.

"Wally . . ."

"Hang on!" I shouted. Since the stream moved slowly, I was able to trot along beside it and keep up. "Don't go anywhere, Wall Street. Don't move."

"That's the problem, Wally. I can't."

"Here we go," Opera shouted over the headset. "You guys are in something called my *bronchioles*. They're a bunch of little passageways that branch off from my windpipe. And that stuff that's waving back and forth, it's called *cilia*."

"Cilia?" I asked.

"Right. And that sticky stream you're talking about, that must be *mucus*."

"Mucus?" Wall Street cried.

"You don't mean that grungy junk we cough up and spit out?" I asked.

"I'm afraid so."

Wall Street shuddered. "I think I'm going to be sick."

Opera kept reading. "It says that the mucus traps foreign particles that enter the lungs and that the cilia push the mucus forward."

"It's another one of our body defenses," I said.

"Yup."

Wall Street was beginning to panic. (I guess the idea of being caught in Opera's mucus didn't thrill her.) She fought harder to get free, but the harder she fought, the deeper she sank—until she was so deep in the stuff it looked like she'd never get out.

Someone had to do something. And since I was the only someone around, it looked like that someone would have to be *this* one. I took a deep breath, swallowed hard, and leaped into the mountain of moving mucus.

For the briefest second, it felt great being the hero. It felt terrific getting to save Wall Street's life for a change. Of course, it might have felt just a little bit greater if, after leaping into the goo, I could have moved my arms. Or my feet. Or any other part of my body. Unfortunately, the goo had me stuck tighter than Scotch tape smothered in Super Glue and topped off with Velcro. The point is I was stuck in a major, I-ain't-going-nowhere-and-I-ain't-going-there-fast kind of way.

"Wally?" Wall Street cried as she looked down and saw me struggling. "What are you doing?"

"I'm saving your life!"

"Oh."

"Just give me time!" I shouted. "I'll get this figured out."

"You can't save me if you're stuck like me."

But that's where she was mistaken. I opened my mouth, ready to set her straight, ready to prove how completely wrong she could be. Unfortunately, the only thing that came out was: "Oh . . . I guess you might be right."

But I wasn't through yet. No way. They don't

call me Wally-the-Disaster-Master for nothing. I bore down for all I was worth. I began kicking and thrashing and squirming. And when that didn't work I tried squirming and thrashing and kicking. Unfortunately, the only thing I managed to free was my left big toe, which really didn't seem all that helpful.

But, oddly enough, it was. For the briefest second that left big toe scraped against the inside of what Opera had called his bronchioles. When it did, there was a series of tremendous explosions, like a half-dozen cannons going off. And with each explosion Wall Street, myself, and the entire river were thrown forward.

Opera was coughing as he shouted over the explosions. "Wally!?"

C-OUGH C-OUGH C-OUGH

And with each cough came another explosion:

K-BOOM, K-BOOM, K-BOOM

and more flying forward.

"OUCH! OUCH! OUCH!"

"What are you doing!?" he cried.

"What am I doing?" I shouted. "What are you doing?!"

He coughed some more.

C-OUGH, C-OUGH, C-OUGH

Which meant more:

K-BOOM, K-BOOM, K-BOOMs

and a lot more flying for us.

"Something's tickling me inside and making me cough!" he cried. "Is it you guys?" He gave a few more hacks, which set off a few more explosions, which meant a few more broken body parts.

Amidst all of the flying and dying, I managed to catch a glimpse of my big toe. Sure enough, it was still sticking out, still wiggling, and still scraping against the side of his bronchioles.

"You might be right," I shouted. "It might be my toe!"

"Well, don't stop!" he shouted back.

"WHAT??"

"According to the readout, that's how we get stuff out of our lungs. We cough it up."

"You don't mean, we're heading—"

He fired off a few more hacks:

C-OUGH, C-OUGH, C-OUGH
K-BOOM, K-BOOM, K-BOOM
"YEOW! OUCH! OUCH!"

"Hang on!" he shouted. "I'm definitely coughing up something."

He continued coughing and wheezing as Wall Street and I continued flying and dying.

"This is it!" Wall Street cried as she shot past me. "We're heading up his windpipe!"

More coughing, more explosions, more flying.

Now it was my turn to sail past her. "Then what!?" I shouted.

More coughing.

Now she was flying past me. "We'll find out when we get there!"

I knew she was right, but I wasn't thrilled about it. I mean here was my one chance to finally be a hero, and I wind up getting killed by being coughed up and spit out of some guy's mouth. It wasn't exactly the ending I'd hoped for. Even now I could imagine the headlines that would be in tomorrow's paper:

Local Youth
Dies as Human Hairball

Yes sir, it wasn't the ending I'd hoped for at all.

Most people dream of going out with a big bang.
I was going out with a wheezing hack.

"Hang on!" Wall Street shouted. "I think I see
the opening up ahead!"

Chapter 10

Wrapping Up

As we shot up Opera's windpipe I could tell we were growing bigger—and we were doing it a lot faster. In fact, it looked like we might not even get out of there in time. I don't want to say I was worried, but I was definitely afraid of giving Opera a new meaning of the phrase, "I've got something caught in my throat."

Wall Street continued pointing to the opening above us. There was a light that was growing bigger and bigger. "It's the back of his mouth!" she shouted. "We're heading up into his mouth!"

Of course she was right. Already we were approaching his tonsils. And just past them, directly in the center, was that pink, dangling, thingama-jigger—you know, that weird piece of flesh that just hangs there in the back of your mouth doing nothing? Well, doing nothing was exactly what Opera's was doing as I raced toward it at a gazillion miles an hour.

"Duck, Wally! Duck!"

I dropped my head and just missed getting clobbered by the soft, meaty stalactite. Wall Street followed right behind.

A moment later we were sailing over a pink, flat something with hundreds of bumps. Of course, it was Opera's tongue (you could tell by the stray potato chip crumbs clinging to it).

Next came his teeth, which had more holes than Swiss cheese (which is what he should have been eating instead of all that junk food).

Then came his lips.

Then came nothing.

Then came nothing!?

I'm afraid so. Suddenly we were freefalling toward the lab floor in a major *I-sure-hope-somebody-catches-me-cause-this-is-going-to-hurt* kind of way.

"AUGH!"

The good news was Opera paid attention to all those health films in school that say we should cover our mouths when coughing. The bad news was that we were growing so fast that by the time we hit his hand, he could barely hold us.

But knowing how allergic I am to dying (I break out in a bad case of death every time it happens), he hung on as all three of us fell to the floor.

"OAFF!"

I tell you, it was great finally seeing the lab again, even if it was from a mouse-size view. Better make that from a cat-size view . . . er, a dog-size view . . . er—well, you get the picture. We were growing faster than a weightlifter on steroids. It only took a few more seconds until we finally reached our original size. And it only took a few more seconds before we were both hugging Opera.

Of course there was the usual, "Oh Opera, I never thought I'd see you alive again," kind of stuff and more than the daily minimum requirement of tears streaming down our faces (though I'm sure mine were from some unknown allergy). Talk about mushy. It was almost as bad as getting hugged by your grandma and all your aunts at one of those family reunions.

We'd probably still be going on like that if it wasn't for the sudden

K-RASH! K-BANG! K-TINKLE!

from the next room.

"What's that?" I cried.

"It's coming from the bathroom," Opera exclaimed. He spun around and took off. We followed right behind. Well, actually, Wall Street followed right behind. It took me a little longer to relearn the fine art of:

K-FALL!
"Ouch!"

walking.

And a little longer than that to:

K-RASH!
"Ow!"
K-SMASH!
"Ooch!"
K-BAMB!
("This is getting embarrassing.")

remember the finer art of NOT walking into walls.

We finally reached the hall leading to the restrooms and came to a screeching halt. Well, Opera and Wall Street came to a screeching halt. I was now relearning how to

K-RASH!

"Ow, watch it Wally!"
"Sorry . . ."

use my brakes.

When I finally pried myself out of the back of my two buddies, I saw the reason for the sudden stop. There, exploding out of the bathroom wall, was the nose of the minisubmarine we'd traveled in.

"What on earth . . ." Wall Street cried.

We continued to watch as the submarine continued to grow, busting out more and more wall until it finally reached its full size, right there in what was left of the bathroom. Of course, it was broken up into dozens of pieces, but there was no mistaking it.

"How'd it get in there?" I asked.

Wall Street shook her head and glanced to Opera. "When we left it, it was still floating around in your intestines."

I nodded. "That's right."

"And since it didn't follow us into your bloodstream, there was no way for it to get out . . ."

I turned to Opera, finishing her thought. "Except . . ."

Opera fidgeted nervously. "I guess I did kind of have to use the bathroom. I mean when I was in there looking for you guys inside my eye."

We all exchanged glances. Now everything made sense. And now I was majorly grateful that we'd found an alternate route of escape.

We finally turned and headed back toward the lab. The rest of the place was still locked up which made it pretty impossible to get out. We cleaned up a bit and, although none of us was crazy about the idea, eventually we decided to call the police . . . who decided to call Mr. Pocket Protector who decided to call our parents . . . who we knew would definitely decide to ground us for life.

But at long last it was over. Of course, we talked about all the cool stuff we had seen and, of course, this made Opera a little embarrassed— after all, we were talking about his insides. But he didn't have to be embarrassed. After all, we were all put together the same way, and it was all pretty awesome.

"It was incredible!" Wall Street said for the hundredth time.

"She's right," I said. "I had no idea how it all worked."

Even Opera was nodding in agreement.

I don't know how long we hung around the lab waiting for the police to show up. But as we waited, I pulled up to the control center Opera had been working from. After a little poking around, I found the computer. It had been quite a while since I'd worked on my Mirror Man story. And, since I wasn't sure the police would let me have a computer while serving my life sentence in the county jail, I figured I better hurry and finish the story now while I had the chance.

I switched on the computer, quickly typed in what I had written earlier in my head, and then I went to work:

When we last left our gorgeously good-looking good guy, his arch villain the rip-roaringly repulsive RetroRunt was exiting a movie theater while preparing to send the world spinning backward again. But why? What is his purpose? Why would he want to do such a notoriously not-so-nice thing? And most importantly, what movie were they going to watch?

Good questions. In fact, they're so good, Mirror Man thinks he'll ask them.

"But why?" he shouts to the mega-midget. "What is your purpose? Why would you want to do such a notoriously not-so-nice thing? And most importantly, what movie are you going to watch?"

(See, I told you so.)

"If you must know, we're going in to
see *The Wizard of Oz,*" the menacing
micro-mite shouts.

"I don't understand," our hero asks,
as he starts toward him. "Why?"

"Stop right there!" RetroRunt cries.
His finger darts to the remote control
on his belt. "One more step and I'll
fire up those retrorockets again!"

Mirror Man slows. But, knowing the
story's coming to an end and knowing
he's the hero who must end it, he con-
tinues forward. "Why this movie,
RetroRunt? Why is it so important you
see *this* movie?"

"Because of all the Munchkins," the
tiny tike answers.

"I still don't understand."

RetroRunt sighs and tries to explain.
"When I watch them, I feel like a normal person."

"But you are normal," Mirror Man
insists.

"You call being so small I have to run
around in the shower just to get wet,
normal?"

"Well no, but——"

"And what about handball? I'm the only

one I know who plays it against street curbs."

"I understand, but——"

"But when I watch all those Munchkins I fit right in. They make me feel good——even if they are the worst singers in the world."

"But the Munchkins, they're only in the first part of the movie."

"Exactly, that's why I keep sending us back in time——so I can watch that same part over and over again."

Now everything begins making sense. (Well, as much sense as any of these superhero stories do.) Desperately, our good guy begins searching for some sort of solution. There must be some way to make this pinky high peewee feel good about himself——some way to convince him to stop using his Retrobelt and making us all relive the same day over and over again. (Of course, our hero could buy him a video of the movie and suggest he keep playing and rewinding it, but money's been a little tight for Mirror Man these days——especially with the rising price of hair spray. Besides, that would be way too boring

of an ending since, as we all know,
superheros are never boring.)

Suddenly, he snaps his fingers. "I've
got it!" he cries. "Let's talk to our
author."

"You don't mean that kid who's writ-
ing this story?"

"Yeah."

"No way. We're make-believe characters. We can't just barge into his
reality like that."

"Why not? He lets his other characters
do it."

"What good would it do?"

"Remember, how he got himself shrunk
by that Miniaturization Machine back
in chapter one?"

"Yeah."

"So let's use that same machine on you."

"But I want to get bigger, not smaller."

"Oh, yeah." Mirror Man scratches his
head. He's obviously stumped. So is
RetroRunt.

"Oh, well," Mirror Man shrugs, "I
guess you're right."

"Oh, well," the flea-high foe sighs as
he reaches for his Retrobelt. "I guess
I am."

I stared at the screen, not believing my eyes. The answer was right there in front of them. And they still couldn't see it. Finally, in frustration, I typed:

"Guys...Guys!"
RetroRunt ducks, looking in all directions for my voice. "Who's there!?" he cries. "Who said that?"

"It's the author," Mirror Man whispers. "I told you he does this sort of thing. Just try and be nice."

RetroRunt clears his tiny little voice and tries a tiny little con act. "Yes, oh Grand and Magnificent one. What does Your Greatness wish?"

"I wish for you to stop trying to butter me up," I typed. Then I continued. **"Can't you guys see the solution here?"**

They exchange uneasy glances.

"Well, I, er..." Mirror Man stutters.
"Um, er, uh..." RetroRunt stalls.

"Come on," I typed, **"if it were any more obvious, it would bite you on the nose."**

"As long as it doesn't leave a nasty red mark," Mirror Man says as he nervously checks his back pocket for his makeup.

"I don't understand," RetroRunt asks.
"What are we supposed to do?"

I explained. "The Miniaturization
Machine makes things small, right?"

"Right," Retro says, "but we want it
to do just the opposite."

"Then use one of Mirror Man's mirrors."

The two look at each other and in perfect unison said, "Huh?"

I rolled my eyes. In the future maybe I should
make my superhero characters a little smarter.
I tried again.

"When you look into the mirror, you
get a perfect reflection, right?"

"Right."

"Except it's just the opposite, right?"

"Right."

"So if you were to shoot the beam into
a mirror at RetroRunt it would have the
same effect, only just the opposite."

Once again they look at each other
and once again they answer in perfect
unison. "Uhhh..."

I'll definitely be making them smarter in the
future. I typed,

"Just trust me on this one, okay?"
"Okay."
"So, can we get on with the story?" I typed.
"You're the boss," RetroRunt says.

I nodded and continued . . .

"Hey," Mirror Man cries. "Don't ask me how, but I've just come up with the perfect solution."

"And what is that?" RetroRunt asks.

"Let's fire the Miniaturization Machine's beam at you through one of my mirrors. It will have the opposite effect. Instead of making you smaller, it will make you bigger."

"Hey, that's a nifty-keen idea, Mirror Man. Why didn't I think of that?"

"Because you're not the hero of this story."

"Oh, yeah, I forgot."

"But come on over to my house. We'll set you up in front of my hundreds of mirrors and fire up the machine. Who knows, by the time we're done you might be tall enough to play for the NBA."

"Well, that would be just superswell of you, Mirror Man."

"That's because I'm a superswell guy. And hey, I bet with a little practice you could become superswell, too."

"Wow, that would be sweller than superswell."

"Well, come on then."

So, as the sun sinks slowly in the west, the two turn and head toward Mirror Man's house. And, once again we can all rest easier knowing that the world will be safer and saner and, although just a bit more boring, a superswell place.

I stopped and looked at the ending. On the McDoogle Corniness Scale of one to ten, it rated somewhere around a fifteen. But that was okay. It was nice to know somebody was having a happy ending. Because as I looked out the lab window and saw the police cars arriving, along with the usual ambulances, fire trucks, TV reporters, and three sets of concerned and very angry parents . . . I knew that a happy ending wouldn't be making any guest appearances on my TV talk show of life.

At least not for a while.

Still, I had learned a few things . . . like never

climb on board minisubmarines without permission—and, if you do, make sure it isn't hovering over an open soda pop can. Then there was that little lesson on how wonderfully and incredibly we're put together. I mean, let's face it, God was definitely having one of his better days when He dreamed us up.

Besides, who knows, if I manage to survive the seventh grade, maybe I'll become a doctor or a biologist or something like that. Of course, that would mean going to college, which would mean Mom and Dad would eventually have to let me off of restriction. Right now the chances of that looked pretty slim, particularly after what we'd just done. But, hey, if God can pull off something as awesome as making our bodies, I bet He can do just about anything.

You'll want to read them all.

THE INCREDIBLE WORLDS OF WALLY McDOOGLE

#1—My Life As a Smashed Burrito with Extra Hot Sauce

Twelve-year-old Wally—"The walking disaster area"—is forced to stand up to Camp Wahkah Wahkah's number one all-American bad guy. One hilarious mishap follows another until, fighting together for their very lives, Wally learns the need for even his worst enemy to receive Jesus Christ. (ISBN 0-8499-3402-8)

#2—My Life As Alien Monster Bait

"Hollyweird" comes to Middletown! Wally's a superstar! A movie company has chosen our hero to be eaten by their mechanical "Mutant from Mars!" It's a close race as to which will consume Wally first—the disaster-plagued special effects "monster" or his own out-of-control pride . . . until he learns the cost of true friendship and of God's command for humility. (ISBN 0-8499-3403-6)

#3—My Life As a Broken Bungee Cord

A hot-air balloon race! What could be more fun? Then again, we're talking about Wally McDoogle, the "Human Catastrophe." Calamity builds on calamity until, with his life on the line, Wally learns what it means to FULLY put his trust in God. (ISBN 0-8499-3404-4)

#4—My Life As Crocodile Junk Food

Wally visits missionary friends in the South American rain forest. Here he stumbles onto a whole new set of impossible predicaments . . . until he understands the need and joy of sharing Jesus Christ with others.
(ISBN 0-8499-3405-2)

#5—My Life As Dinosaur Dental Floss

It starts with a practical joke that snowballs into near disaster. Risking his life to protect his country, Wally is pursued by a SWAT team, bungling terrorists, photo-snapping tourists, Gary the Gorilla, and a TV news reporter. After prehistoric-size mishaps and a talk with the President, Wally learns that maybe honesty really is the best policy. (ISBN 0-8499-3537-7)

#6—My Life As a Torpedo Test Target

Wally uncovers the mysterious secrets of a sunken submarine. As dreams of fame and glory increase, so do the famous McDoogle mishaps. Besides hostile sea creatures, hostile pirates, and hostile Wally McDoogle clumsiness, there is the war against his own greed and selfishness. It isn't until Wally finds himself on a wild ride atop a misguided torpedo that he realizes the source of true greatness. (ISBN 0-8499-3538-5)

#7—My Life As a Human Hockey Puck

Look out . . . Wally McDoogle turns athlete! Jealousy and envy drive Wally from one hilarious calamity to another until, as the team's mascot, he learns humility while suddenly being thrown in to play goalie for the Middletown Super Chickens! (ISBN 0-8499-3601-2)

#8—My Life As an Afterthought Astronaut

"Just cause I didn't follow the rules doesn't make it my fault that the Space Shuttle almost crashed. Well, okay, maybe it was sort of my fault. But not the part when Pilot O'Brien was spacewalking and I accidently knocked him halfway to Jupiter. . . ." So begins another hilarious Wally McDoogle MISadventure as our boy blunder stows aboard the Space Shuttle and learns the importance of: Obeying the Rules!
(ISBN 0-8499-3602-0)

#9—My Life As Reindeer Road Kill

Santa on an out-of-control four wheeler? Electrical Rudolph on the rampage? Nothing unusual, just Wally McDoogle doing some last-minute Christmas shopping . . . FOR GOD! Our boy blunder dreams that an angel has invited him to a birthday party for Jesus. Chaos and comedy follow as he turns the town upside down looking for the perfect gift, until he finally bumbles his way into the real reason for the Season. (ISBN 0-8499-3866-X)

#10—My Life As a Toasted Time Traveler

Wally travels back from the future to warn himself of an upcoming accident. But before he knows it, there are more Wallys running around than even Wally himself can handle. Catastrophes reach an all-time high as Wally tries to out-think God and re-write history. (ISBN 0-8499-3867-8)

#11—My Life As Polluted Pond Scum

This laugh-filled Wally disaster includes: a monster lurking in the depths of a mysterious lake . . . a glowing figure with powers to summon the creature to the shore . . . and one Wally McDoogle, who reluctantly stumbles upon the truth. Wally's entire town is in danger. He must race against the clock, his own fears, and learn to trust God before he has any chance of saving the day. (ISBN 0-8499-3875-9)

#12—My Life As a Bigfoot Breath Mint

Wally gets his big break to star with his uncle Max in the famous Fantasmo World stunt show. Unlike his father, whom Wally secretly suspects to be a major loser, Uncle Max is everything Wally longs to be . . . or so it appears. But Wally soon discovers the truth and learns who the real hero is in his life. (ISBN 0-8499-3876-7)

#13—My Life As a Blundering Ballerina

Wally agrees to switch places with Wall Street. Everyone is in on the act as the two try to survive seventy-two hours in each other's shoes and learn the importance of respecting other people. (ISBN 0-8499-4022-2)

#14—My Life As a Screaming Skydiver

Master of mayhem Wally turns a game of laser tag into international espionage. From the Swiss Alps to the African plains, Agent 00½th bumblingly employs such top-secret gizmos as rocket-powered toilet paper, exploding dental floss, and the ever-popular transformer tacos to stop the dreaded and super secret . . . Giggle Gun. (ISBN 0-8499-4023-0)

#15—My Life As a Human Hairball

When Wally and Wall Street visit a local laboratory, they are accidentally miniaturized and swallowed by some unknown stranger. It is a race against the clock as they fly through various parts of the body in a desperate search for a way out while learning how wonderfully we're made. (ISBN 0-8499-4024-9)

#16—My Life As a Walrus Whoopee Cushion

Wally and his buddies, Opera and Wall Street, win the Gazillion Dollar Lotto! Everything is great, until they realize they lost the ticket at the zoo! Add some bungling bad guys, a zoo break-in, the release of all the animals, a SWAT team or two . . . and you have the usual McDoogle mayhem as Wally learns the dangers of greed. (ISBN 0-8499-4025-7)

#17—My Life As a Mixed-up Millennium Bug

When Wally accidently fries the circuits of Ol' Betsy, his beloved laptop computer, suddenly whatever he types turns into reality! At 11:59, New Year's Eve, Wally tries retyping the truth into his computer—which shorts out every other computer in the world. By midnight, the entire universe has credited Wally's mishap to the MILLENNIUM BUG! Panic, chaos, and hilarity start the new century, thanks to our beloved boy blunder. (ISBN 0-8499-4026-5)

#18—My Life As a Beat-Up Basketball Backboard

Ricko Slicko's Advertising Agency claims that they can turn the dorkiest human in the world into the most popular. And who better to prove this than our boy blunder, Wally McDoogle! Soon he has his own TV series and fans wearing glasses just like his. But when he tries to be a star athlete for his school basketball team, Wally finally learns that being popular isn't all it's cut out to be. (ISBN 0-8499-4027-3)

Would You Like To Interview

Bill Myers
In Your Classroom?

If your class has access to a speaker
phone, you can interview Bill Myers,
author of The Incredible Worlds of Wally
McDoogle series—which has sold over
2 million copies—and The Imager
Chronicles series. You'll be able to ask
him about his life as a writer and how
he created the famous boy blunder
and the land of Fayrah.

It's Fun!
It's Easy!
It's Educational!

For information, just have your
teacher e-mail us at
Tommy Nelson® and ask for details!
E-mail: prdept@tommynelson.com